Late that night, w... ...ough-
out the city, Matt w... ...ts, trying
to decide what to do.

There was something awesomely beautiful
yet painfully sad about the tall, empty
buildings glowing in the firelight. Matt
gazed at the structures and marvelled at the
towering monuments to the ability of man.
Yet man had really flopped when it had
counted . . .

FIREBRATS

SHOCKWAVE

Barbara Siegel & Scott Siegel

Methuen

First published in the United States 1988
by Simon & Schuster, Inc
First published in Great Britain 1988
as a Methuen Teens paperback
by Methuen Children's Books
A Division of OPG Services Limited
Michelin House, 81 Fulham Road, London SW3 6RB
Copyright © 1988 Siegel & Siegel Ltd
Printed in Great Britain
by Cox & Wyman Ltd, Reading

ISBN 0 416 04552 9

To Steve Moisoff—

For his support, insight, and compassion.
During the worst of times,
he was the best of friends.

SHOCKWAVE

Chapter 1

WHAT MONTH IS IT?" ASKED MATT CHANDLER AS HE rode his horse, Herbie, along the broken, weed-strewn interstate highway.

"July, I think," Dani replied uncertainly, gazing at the endless reddish-purple clouds above.

Matt shrugged. "That's what I thought, too. I guess it's warmer than it used to be, but it sure isn't summer."

"I wonder if we'll ever see summer again?" Dani wondered with a mournful sigh as they continued to trudge west on their tired horses.

The nuclear war had changed everything—the land, the sky, and even the seasons. It had also changed Matt and Dani. Matt was just shy of seventeen, but he had grown up fast. It was either that or die in the rubble that had once been America. He knew it and so did his pretty, dark-haired companion, Dani Cortland. She had been a high school student and an aspiring actress. But all she aspired to now was survival.

Matt and Dani had met for the first time on the very day their safe, secure world was shattered. They had been together ever since, slowly making their way westward, hoping to find Matt's family, his mom and dad, who had been in California visiting his brother the night the missiles hit.

"If it's July," said Matt, thinking back to a way of life that no longer existed, "then school would be over and I'd be working at McDonald's. And maybe you'd walk in with a couple of your girlfriends," he added, smiling at Dani, trying to cheer her up.

"What I wouldn't give for a Big Mac, fries, and a Diet Coke," she said wistfully.

"You'd walk up to the counter and our eyes would meet," Matt continued.

"Maybe I'd get two Big Macs."

"Are you listening to me?"

"Huh? Oh, yeah, sure," she replied absently.

"Well, I'd just be finishing my shift and I'd ask you to ditch your friends and go see a movie with me. And you'd say—"

"I'd get the large fries. No doubt about it."

"Dani!"

"What?"

"Stop talking about food. I'm trying to take you out."

It was a game they often played, imagining what their lives would have been like had the war never happened. They always ended up on a date—the movies, bowling, roller-skating—but neither of them ever fantasized about the end of the evening—at least

2

not out loud. It was a never-ending date with both of them wondering if it would climax with a passionate kiss good night—or a slap in the face.

"I'm sorry," said Dani. "I just can't get into it. We haven't eaten since we finished those wild potatoes yesterday, and I'm getting scared. There's nothing growing around here that's edible."

Matt nodded, then automatically scanned the high plains they were riding through. The land was flat and barren without the endless fields of wheat that had once carpeted the ground.

But then his gaze riveted on something far in the western distance.

"You see that?" Matt asked, pointing to a dark speck on the side of the road up ahead.

Dani squinted and stared. "There's something there, all right," she agreed.

"Maybe it's a giant Big Mac," teased Matt.

"I'd settle for just the lettuce and the pickles," said Dani. "Come on, let's check it out."

After riding a few more miles they identified what they had seen. It was a dilapidated truck stop. When they got still closer, they noticed a few rusting cars and trucks in the big parking lot. The doors, trunks, and hoods were open or missing on the cars. The trucks had also been scavenged. And the truck stop itself hadn't fared much better. The windows were broken and the front door was hanging by a single hinge. The building, a relic of the past, looked as if it was haunted.

They had passed such places before—dozens of

times. They were always stripped clean of anything even faintly useful.

"Want to go inside and look around?" Matt asked anyway.

Dani shook her head. "Why bother?"

"You never know," Matt doggedly replied. "Maybe there's still a can of Spam or a box of cough drops lying around."

"We never find anything in truck stops," she complained.

"There's always a first time."

"There's a first time for starving, too," Dani said irritably. "I say we keep going. Maybe we'll find a pond or a lake. Then we can catch a fish or cook up some cattails. Besides, it's the middle of the day. We can put a lot of miles behind us if we just keep going."

In the past travelers had pulled into the old truck stop to buy gas, have a meal, and use the bathroom. But no more. The old ways were over. There were no more trucks and no more stops to make.

Matt and Dani rode on, passing it by.

They hadn't gone far, however, when Dani shivered, turned back to Matt, and said, "Temperature's dropping, isn't it?"

Matt was about to answer when he heard something go *thunk* on the ground just to his right. He twisted in his saddle to look. At the same time Herbie lifted his ears. "You heard it, too, didn't you?" he whispered to the animal.

Thunk.

This time the sound was on the left side of the road.

And it was loud. Dani, who had been riding just ahead of Matt, heard it and reined her horse in. "What kind of creature makes a noise like that?" she asked, fear rising in her voice.

"I don't know," Matt said. "But if it's an animal, there's more than one of them." With one hand, he started to lift his bow from around his shoulders. With the other, he reached for an arrow from his quiver.

Thunk. Thunk.

"They're ahead of us," cried Dani.

"No, they're behind us," said Matt, nocking an arrow into his bowstring. But he had no idea what he was going to shoot at.

Both horses were panicking. It was hard to hold them steady.

Thunk. Thunk. Thunk.

A harsh, cold wind began to blow. Matt and Dani tried to ignore the bitter chill while they searched all around for a horde of menacing animals.

Crack!

That was loud and different. Matt and Dani turned toward the place from which that sound had come. Right between their two horses, they saw it. There, rolling on the concrete of the highway, was a hailstone almost the size of a baseball!

Thunk. Thunk. Crack!

The hailstones were just starting to come down, hitting the hard-packed ground and roadway like small bombs. And they were just as dangerous. Those balls of ice could kill—at the very least, maim.

5

"We've got to find shelter!" Matt shouted, thrusting his bow over his shoulder.

"The truck stop!" said Dani, turning Whisk around to gallop back the way they had come.

Matt was right behind her.

The truck stop wasn't very far away. But the weather was unrelenting. The hailstones came plummeting down out of the sky in greater numbers with every passing second.

One of the ice balls hit Herbie square in the rump. The horse stumbled and nearly fell over. Matt steadied him, and Herbie ran as fast as he could, a wild look in his eyes.

Thunk. Crack! Thunk. Thunk. Crack!

A piece of ice grazed Matt's left arm. His forearm immediately felt numb despite the fact it had only been a glancing blow.

He kept on riding.

Dani took a ricochet from a hailstone that bounced up off the roadway, smashing into her heel and instep. If she hadn't been partially protected by the stirrup, she knew it would have broken her foot.

They raced off the highway and down the service road that led to the truck stop. They were only a hundred yards away. Maybe less.

And that was when the sky opened up!

The huge, deadly hailstones struck the ground and the highway so often that they sounded like a drummer gone berserk. And Matt and Dani knew—with a terrible certainty—that they'd never reach the truck stop alive.

Chapter 2

A HAILSTONE HIT MATT ON THE BACK AND KNOCKED him off his horse. The only luck he had was in not crashing onto the service road. Instead he fell on the slightly softer earth at the road's shoulder. Still, he had suffered a hard blow and a bad fall. When the initial shock wore off, he would be left with a badly bruised back. But at least now he could move.

Herbie had run away, and Matt was alone as he struggled to his feet. When he looked up, he saw Dani riding back to help him.

"No! Keep going!" he shouted, waving his arms at her, trying to tell her to save herself. Dani either didn't hear Matt or just ignored him. She rode toward him as gigantic hailstones crashed and bounced all around.

Dani reined Whisk in just a few feet from Matt. The horse reared up when a hailstone hit its right foreleg. Dani held on, quickly settled Whisk down, then reached for Matt's hand.

"Climb up! Hurry!" she cried.

Matt was just about to pull himself up in the saddle behind her when a hailstone slammed against the side of Dani's head.

Blood suddenly covered her temple and ran down her cheek as she slumped over and fell toward Matt. Caught off guard, and dizzy himself, Matt couldn't catch her. In fact, her limp body knocked him down and the two of them went sprawling.

Whisk had seen and felt enough; the horse took off after Herbie. Dani was out cold, but she had the end of Whisk's reins wrapped around her wrist. When the horse turned and bolted, it started dragging her. Matt scrambled into a run and then dove at the reins, grabbing hold of them just above Dani's wrist. That slowed Whisk down, but it didn't stop him. The horse dragged both of them along the cracked, uneven service road, into the truck stop's parking lot.

While the roadway ripped at the front of their bodies, the hailstones pelted their backs. The best that Matt could do was to try to protect their heads with his one free arm.

Matt had no idea where Whisk was taking them. For all he knew, the horse was running wild. But he knew one thing for certain: They couldn't take the pounding much longer. They were being slowly stoned to death by nature.

As they were dragged toward an abandoned car, Matt wrestled his knife free from the sheath on his belt and cut the reins just above Dani's wrist. They came to an abrupt stop as Whisk galloped free of them.

8

They were just a few yards from the rusting car.

Matt picked Dani up in his arms and ran with her, throwing her into the car's back seat. Then he dove in beside her.

Grapefruit-size hailstones smashed against the hood; the sound was deafening. Some of the hailstones bounced inside through the open doorways and shattered the back window and front windshield. But the ricocheting chunks of ice didn't have the same lethal force as the ones that were direct hits.

They were out of the worst of it. Matt just hoped that Dani would be all right.

He took a hailstone from the floor of the car, scraped off a small chunk of ice, and when it melted in his hands, he cleaned the cut on Dani's temple with the cold water. Once the blood and dirt were washed away, he saw that the cut wasn't very deep. She had taken an awful bang on the head, though, and the bruised area was sure to become badly swollen.

Well, he thought with a grim smile, *at least there's plenty of ice to keep the swelling down.* He took off his Fair Oaks High School jacket and then stripped out of his shirt. He trembled, put the jacket back on, and snapped it up to his neck. Then, wrapping one of the hailstones in his shirt, Matt held it against Dani's bruised head.

While he sat quietly in the car taking care of Dani, the world around him was heaving with misery. The wind howled, and huge hailstones tumbled out of the sky, trying to level the earth and wipe it clean—as if God wanted to make a fresh start.

9

The hailstorm was at its height when Dani's eyes opened. She slowly focused on Matt's face—and she smiled.

Matt smiled back.

"How do you feel?" he asked over the sound of the hail crashing into the car, denting every inch of it.

"Glad to wake up," she said hoarsely. "When I got hit, I felt myself falling. I thought it was all over for me. End of the road."

"Can't always believe your first impressions," Matt said lightly.

Dani tried to sit up and groaned. "Well, I know I'm alive because I hurt all over."

"I know. I feel the same way. It reminds me of when I was little and I got into a dirt bomb fight with my friend, Cliff. He—"

"What's a dirt bomb?" she interrupted.

"You know, a clump of dirt, like a snowball. When it hits you, the dirt kind of explodes in every direction." He shrugged, not sure if he was making himself clear. "Anyway," he said, "we always called them dirt bombs."

"So?"

"So, sometimes there were rocks inside the dirt bombs. And I hit Cliff with one of those by accident. He got real mad and started throwing rocks at me. Hit me a few times, too. I was black and blue for a week."

"We'll be black and blue for a lot longer this time," said Dani.

"Yeah. And over a lot more of our bodies."

With help from Matt, Dani managed to sit up. He

kept his arm around her to keep her warm, and because he liked how it felt.

They were both staring out through the shattered front windshield, watching hailstones clatter against the car's hood.

"It's sort of like we're at a drive-in movie," said Dani. "You know, sitting in the back seat, looking out, watching the show."

"I thought the show was always inside the car," quipped Matt.

Dani chuckled. "Yeah, it usually was. I remember once when—"

"I don't want to hear it," Matt said suddenly.

Surprised, Dani said, "Hey, you told me your dirt-bomb story. Why can't I tell you mine?"

"I—I just don't want to hear it," he muttered.

Dani gave Matt a dirty look and turned her face away from him. Then it dawned on her; he was jealous! She started giggling.

"What's so funny?" Matt asked defensively.

"Nothing. I was just thinking."

"About what?"

"About how I ditched my girlfriends and left McDonald's with you to go out on a date. And here we are at a drive-in movie."

Matt brightened. "What's the flick?" he asked, playing along.

Dani made believe she was peering out at the movie screen. "Looks like *Attack of the Killer Hailstones,*" she said.

He laughed. "I heard that was real good."

11

"Yeah, well, you're the guy who thought *The Good, the Bad, and the Thirsty* was a great film."

"Only after the hero and heroine found water," he reminded her.

"And how are the hero and the heroine going to make it out of *this* mess? They don't have any food, they don't know where their horses are—if they're still alive—and they're stuck in the middle of nowhere, beat-up, bruised, and cold."

"Sounds pretty gruesome," he admitted. And it was. He was scared that their journey—and their lives—were about to come to an end. There was no way, though, that he'd admit that to Dani. He put on a brave face and said, "You know, when the movie is scary, the girl is supposed to cling real close to the guy."

He hugged her.

She hugged him back, hoping to find her courage in his arms.

"Matt?" she finally whispered.

"Yeah?"

"Would you get me some popcorn?"

Chapter 3

WHEN THE HAILSTORM FINALLY ENDED, MATT AND Dani crawled out of the back seat of the car onto a field of ice that was more than a foot deep.

"Looks like about a zillion super-big ice-cube trays got emptied on top of us," said Matt.

"And I feel like every single one of them hit me," added Dani.

They balanced themselves on top of the hailstones and walked precariously toward the truck stop. The old building would provide them with better shelter than the back seat of the car; it would be warmer there, and they could stretch out and move around. Besides, they knew they weren't going anywhere until the ice melted. They could—and had—traveled on snow, but ice was another matter. Especially as they had lost their horses and had to continue their journey on foot.

Matt slipped and fell three times, Dani twice, before they reached the building's main entrance. The storm had knocked the door off its final hinge and it now lay buried under the hail.

They entered the truck stop and looked around. There was a Coke machine lying on its side, the front of it ripped away. There were no soda cans left inside. The same held true for a snack machine. The front glass had been smashed off yet another machine that sold cheap little knickknacks, such as packages of tissues, playing cards, and whistles. Matt carefully reached in past the shards of glass and pulled out a green plastic comb.

"My father always said that going out without your hair combed was like going out without having your pants on," Matt said softly. "I can't wait to get to California. He'll get a kick out of it when I pull out this comb and run it through my hair."

Dani bit her lip to keep from crying. California had never seemed farther away. "Come on," she said gruffly, forcing back her tears. "Let's look around."

The dining room was empty. There were no tables or chairs—not even a bit of carpet. All of that had probably been burned for heat. They knew they were wasting their time, but they checked out the kitchen, looking for any scrap of food they might find.

They were right. They had wasted their time.

"At least there'll be plenty of water to drink while the hail melts," Matt said.

Dani wasn't particularly thrilled at the prospect of an all-water diet. She walked over to a shattered dining room window and looked out.

She was startled when a dark shadow moved at the far edge of the left side of her vision.

"Matt!" she cried. "There's something out there!"

He ran to the doorway to get a better look. His mind was racing with possibilities. None of them good. There could be scavengers out there, or maybe a wild, hungry animal driven toward the smell of food— meaning Dani and him.

"What is it?" Dani called out anxiously. "Can you see?"

"I can't believe it!" he shouted back.

"Tell me!"

"It's Herbie and Whisk!" he announced. "They're alive!"

Dani bolted from the window, cheering and sobbing at the same time. She skidded up next to Matt amid the already melting hailstones at the doorway. He grabbed her to keep her from falling. Then they held each other, watching as Herbie and Whisk stuck their heads out of the shadowed open bay of the truck stop's service area to gingerly lick at the hailstones. They had obviously saved themselves by taking refuge in the garage.

Their horses meant much more to Matt and Dani than just transportation. Herbie and Whisk were their friends, the ones to whom they told their secrets when they were afraid to share them with each other. Only Herbie knew how Matt truly felt about Dani. And only Whisk knew what Dani felt about Matt. The horses had heard it all, listening without complaining, never giving useless advice, and always ready with a loving lick on the cheek to wipe away salty tears.

Now their friends, whom they had feared either dead or lost, had reappeared. Matt and Dani might have empty stomachs, but at least their hearts were full.

They hurriedly stumbled across the ice-covered parking lot to the animals, who had been badly cut and bruised by the ice and were in need of some tender loving care.

The horses had been in a sweat and were now in danger of catching cold. Matt and Dani quickly unsaddled them and dried them off. They had some salve in their saddlebags and carefully applied it to the horses' open wounds.

The animals stoically stood still while they were attended to. At least they weren't terribly hungry. They had regularly grazed on the short grass along the highway before the hailstorm, and they could hold out until the ice melted. It was going to be a lot tougher for Matt and Dani to do without food.

Matt closed one of the service area's bay doors to protect the horses from the wind. The other door was gone. Then Matt and Dani picked up their saddlebags and carried them back to the main building to settle in for the night.

The moon and the stars had been hidden from view ever since the night of the war. When the sun went down behind the ever-present cloud cover, total darkness shrouded the land.

Matt and Dani had run out of candles a long time before, and the matches they still had were hoarded as if they were gold. As soon as the darkness descended, they curled up next to each other in a corner of the large dining room. Using their saddlebags for pillows, they said their good-nights.

Exhausted from their harrowing day, they both fell asleep quickly. And deeply—until a sharp noise, like the sound of a door slamming, suddenly shocked them awake.

"Did you hear that?" Matt whispered in the blackness.

Dani's fingers digging into his arm told him that it had been a stupid question.

"Maybe something fell," he said hopefully. "The storm could have shaken things loose, you know?"

Dani took a deep breath to calm herself. "Yeah. You're probably right." She slowly exhaled.

They lay down again and closed their eyes.

Before they fell asleep, though, they heard a creaking sound but Matt figured it was caused by the wind blowing through the dilapidated old building. Dani shivered, but not because of the cold.

"Relax," Matt whispered in her ear.

"I guess I'm not used to sleeping with a roof over my head." She sighed. "I feel kind of closed in—trapped."

"You just have to get used to the sounds," said Matt softly, reassuring her.

"I know. I guess I just have a vivid imagination."

"How do you mean?"

17

"Well, just a second ago I could have sworn I heard a floorboard creak. It sounded like a footstep," she said, feeling foolish.

Matt smiled in the darkness. "I heard it, too. Don't worry about it. It's just the wind." There was a prankster part of him that wanted to lean close to her and shout, "Boo." But there was another part that only wanted to put his arms around her and protect her.

He felt her body tremble.

"Hey, come on," he said gently. "Everything's okay. You just got spooked by that noise before. Forget it and go to sleep."

Matt massaged the back of her neck and her shoulders.

"I like that," she said with a purr in her voice. She leaned in closer to him, snuggling for warmth—of every kind.

This isn't bad, Matt thought to himself. *I wish she got scared more often.*

While Matt gently rubbed her back, Dani finally dozed off. Feeling his eyes drooping, Matt lowered his head to join her in sleep. But then floorboards creaked again. And this time it was followed by a distinct scuffing sound. And then another creak—and another. Matt couldn't breathe. Dani *had* been right.

Footsteps.

And they were getting close!

Chapter 4

IT WAS PITCH BLACK, BUT MATT COULD TELL BY THE sound that it was no animal that was stalking them. It was a human.

Matt covered Dani's mouth with one hand and unsheathed his knife with the other. "Keep quiet," he whispered as Dani bolted awake. "We've got company."

Dani was scared, but somehow not so afraid as she had been earlier. Now that there was something tangible to fear, there was also something tangible to fight. She unsheathed her own knife, and like Matt, she scrambled into a crouch, ready for anything.

The footsteps sounded hesitant and uncertain in the darkness.

Matt strained to listen. The sound bounced off the walls of the empty building, and it was hard to pinpoint the exact location of the stalker.

"The kitchen," whispered Dani.

Her sense of hearing was better than his, and Matt trusted that she was right.

They had been wise to bed down in a corner of the dining room. With a corner at their backs, no one could sneak up on them from behind. Facing whoever was in front of them was scary enough.

"How many?" questioned Matt in a thin, low voice.

Dani hesitated, listening, then leaned closer to Matt and whispered in his ear, "Sounds like only one."

Footsteps crunched on broken glass.

Sweat dripped off Matt's forehead into his right eye. He rubbed it away with his left hand and clutched the knife in his right even tighter.

From the sound of the footsteps, this Phantom of the Truck Stop couldn't have been more than fifteen feet away.

Suddenly there was a loud bump, and a voice cried out, "Ow!" A long, colorful string of swear words flew out of a man's mouth.

It was now obvious to Matt and Dani that the stranger didn't know they were there. That gave them the advantage of surprise. Matt figured they'd better use that advantage before the stranger stumbled upon them and attacked them out of fear.

In the deepest voice he could muster, so he wouldn't sound like a kid, Matt called out, "Don't come any closer!"

There was an audible gasp. The man obviously stumbled backward and fell to the floor as if he'd been shot. "Who's there?" he asked in shocked surprise.

It worked. "Never mind," said Matt. "Just back off."

"Sure—sure—uh, but I can't see where I'm going," said the stranger nervously, feeling his way backward. He bumped into something and swore again.

"Where did you come from?" demanded Matt, no longer afraid of the man in the darkness.

"Never you mind," he said sharply in return. "It's none of your business. You want to sleep in the dining room? Fine. I'll stay out of your way. You stay out of mine. I'm going."

"Wait a minute," Dani called out.

"There's more than one of you?" the man asked anxiously, his voice still moving away from them.

"Never *you* mind," Dani said back like a shot. There was no telling if this guy had friends somewhere. The less he knew about them, the better. "You said we could stay in the dining room," she questioned. "How did you know this was a dining room? Have you been here before?"

The stranger emitted a nervous laugh. But he wouldn't answer. The farther he crawled away from Matt and Dani, the calmer he became. "You'll get all your answers in the morning," he said mysteriously. "And so will I."

They heard him climb to his feet and listened to the sound of his receding footsteps. A door closed, and then they heard nothing at all.

He was gone.

But where?

At first Matt and Dani both stayed awake in case the stranger came back. As the night wore on, though, they became exhausted.

"Maybe we should keep watch in shifts," Matt finally suggested.

Dani yawned. "Good idea. I'll take the first shift." She yawned again. "I'll wake you up when I get sleepy."

"You're already sleepy," Matt said. "It's nice of you to offer, but you really don't have to. Why don't you rest now, and I'll wake you up in a little while. Okay?"

Dani didn't answer; she was fast asleep.

At dawn Matt and Dani hoisted their saddlebags over their shoulders and left the main building. It was warmer than they had expected it to be, and they found the hailstones were already more than half melted.

They slogged through the slush to check on their horses in the truck stop's service area. They didn't want the stranger from the night before to find their horses first.

Herbie nickered as they approached. He was glad to see his two human friends and was hoping they had some food with them.

No such luck.

The horses seemed to be healing well from their cuts and bruises of the day before. After cleaning the wounds again and putting on a new layer of fresh salve, Matt and Dani turned to head back to the main building.

They each took one step toward the open bay door of the service area and then stopped dead in their tracks.

An old man stood in the doorway. He was frail-looking and didn't seem particularly threatening—except for the pistol he held in his hands.

"So you're the two who scared ten years off my life last night," the old man said amiably enough while pointing the pistol in Matt and Dani's direction.

"I guess so," Matt replied evenly, angry at himself for not guarding the door.

"Been watching you," said the old man. "You treat those horses real well."

Matt nodded. He didn't know what to say.

"I've lived out here in Colorado a long time now," said the old man, scratching at a scraggly beard as he spoke. "Most folks who owned land usually kept themselves some horses, too. 'Course, that's all changed now. But I usually found that the nice folks took good care of their horses, and the miserable folks treated their horses real mean. It's not a hard and fast rule, but it mostly seemed to work that way. So, I'm figuring you two kids are decent folks."

"Then why don't you put down your gun?" asked Dani.

"Like I said, it's not a hard and fast rule."

"The way I see it," said Matt thoughtfully, "you could have shot us already if you'd wanted to. So you're probably a good guy. How can we prove to you that we're good guys, too?"

"One at a time, each of you take your knives out of your scabbards—use just two fingers—and drop the blades on the ground," he said. "Then kick them over toward me."

23

They did as they were told.

The old man lowered his gun—but he didn't put it away. "My name is Sarge Podlawski," he said. "Who are you and what are you doing here?"

Matt and Dani told him their names. Then Dani said, "We had already passed this truck stop but came back when the hailstorm started. What about you? What are you doing here?"

Podlawski smiled broadly, showing rotted teeth. "Me? I've always been here. I was the cook at this truck stop. Everybody figured this whole area would get incinerated in the war. After all, we're only one hundred miles from the Denver city limits. So, when the first alert came, the place emptied out real fast."

"Why didn't you leave?" asked Matt.

"Where would I go?" retorted Podlawski. "Where did any of them truckers go? They drove out of here at a hundred-twenty miles per hour heading due east, away from Denver. Had my CB unit on, listening to them jabber on the airwaves. It was disgusting. Half of them ended up in wrecks trying to pass each other on the road. And from what I could make out, they drove right into a firestorm, 'cause I heard a couple of screams before everything went dead."

"How did *you* survive?" questioned Matt.

"The storage area for the truck stop is in the basement," Podlawski explained. "Whatever I needed that wasn't already there, I brought down. Then I boarded up the stairway and stayed in the basement for two months before coming up to look around.

Since then, I come topside every few nights for a little air. It's safer at night 'cause nobody can see anything. Most of the time, though, I stay underground so I don't have to worry about any marauders coming by. But to tell you the truth, I thought I bought the farm last night. You really surprised me."

"Have you been alone all this time?" asked Dani, peering into the sad, sunken eyes of the old man.

"Just me and the rats," said Podlawski. "But the rats ain't been farin' that well lately. I'm getting to be a pretty good shot. Hate wasting the ammo on them, though, but what are you going to do, huh?"

"You could leave," suggested Matt. "You must be running low on food by now. And you can't stay here forever, living all alone."

"Who said I can't?" demanded the old man. "It's the first time in my whole life I've been my own boss. I eat when I want, sleep when I want, and I don't have a lick of work to do that I don't want to do. Does that sound bad to you?"

"It sounds awfully lonely," offered Dani.

"Missy," said Podlawski, "I'm seventy-four years old. I've been around people all my life, a good part of it in the army. And let me tell you, I've had my fill of people. I've cooked for them for more than fifty years, as a mess sergeant in the service and as a short-order cook here at the truck stop. I fed my share of jerks and dopes. And let me tell you, I'm glad to be done with them."

"But what about when you run out of food?" Dani asked, persisting. "What will you do then?"

25

The old man laughed harshly. "I'll die," he said simply. "Just like everybody else."

Matt suddenly felt a chill. It sounded as if the old man knew something that they didn't know. "You said you had a CB radio," Matt said. "Have you heard anything about California? Are people still alive out there?"

"CB never worked after that night," he said with a shrug. "I have no idea what's left out there. No idea at all."

"Aren't you curious?" asked Matt.

"Nope. Like I said, my life ain't too bad compared to most, and 'compared to most' is how folks generally figure their success in life. I used to be a poor man 'compared to most,' but now I'm doing just fine. Not that I couldn't be doing a little better." There was an edge to the old man's voice that put Matt and Dani on their guard.

"What do you mean?" asked Matt.

"Life's been good and I mean to keep it that way. I figure I could use some fresh meat. Horse meat. I think I'd like that one." He pointed his pistol at Herbie.

Chapter 5

"DON'T SHOOT!" MATT SHOUTED, JUMPING IN FRONT OF his horse.

Startled, the old man lowered his pistol. "I wasn't going to kill your horse—at least not yet," said Podlawski. "I was just telling you which one I wanted. I've always been fair with folks, and I'll be fair with you, too. I'm willing to trade for that horse, and I'll tell you what I'll offer. I'll give you two sixty-four-ounce cans of fruit cocktail, a five-pound can of applesauce, a five-pound bag of flour, two bottles of Yoo-Hoo chocolate drink, and I'll even throw in a pack of Dentyne chewing gum. What do you say?"

"We're not trading Herbie for food," Matt said flatly.

"What's the big deal?" asked Podlawski. "You'll still have your other horse to eat."

"We're not going to eat Whisk, either," said Dani, rubbing her horse on the neck.

The old man shook his head with disgust. "If you don't have anything else to eat, you'll eat those horses

27

and enjoy every bite," he said. "But that's neither
here nor there. Those horses look like the only things
of value you've got. If you want to trade for some
food, you'd better come up with something I want."
Feigning indifference, he shrugged his shoulders and
said, "Of course, maybe you don't want to trade with
me at all. If that's how it is, it's no skin off my nose."
He casually turned and started to leave.

"Wait," Matt said quickly, his stomach rumbling.
"We'd really like to trade with you. Just give us a
second, okay?"

Podlawski stopped and smirked. Knowing that they
were eager meant that he could drive a hard bargain.

"What have you got?" the old man demanded.

Matt and Dani opened their saddlebags and
dumped everything they owned out on the floor. It
wasn't much. A brush for the horses, a half a bar of
soap, two forks, two spoons, two tin plates, a collaps-
ible aluminum pot, a frying pan, three plastic water
bottles, two empty backpacks, a box of matches, and
an extra change of clothes for each of them.

"That's all?" asked Podlawski.

Matt turned and gestured at their two saddles.
"We've got those," he said. "Plus my bow and a
quiver full of arrows, a couple of canteens, and some
rope."

The old man made a face. "The bow and arrows
might be worth something to somebody, but not to
me." He lifted the barrel of the pistol to make his
point. "As for the rest of that stuff, I don't need any of
it. I've got a ten-gallon container of liquid soap that'd

last me a lifetime even if I was your age. The last thing a truck stop needs are silverware, plates, and pots. Your clothes ain't going to fit me. And a saddle and a horse brush are a waste without a horse to use them on. So it looks like you two are a little short in the trading department."

"You didn't mention the rope," said Matt. "Maybe you could use that."

"Nope," said Podlawski. "Can always use electrical wire for tying things up."

"What about the matches?" asked Dani, picking up the small box from underneath her extra shirt.

"We need those," said Matt, shaking his head at Dani.

As she started to put them back down, the old man said, "Just a minute. I might be willing to trade a little something for those matches. They're not worth much, and I don't really need them, but they'd be good to have around."

"We can't trade the matches," Matt insisted.

"It's up to you," said Podlawski easily. "But you can't let yourselves starve, either."

"He's right," Dani conceded. "We can keep a few matches for emergencies and trade the rest. The matches aren't going to do us any good if we're dead."

"All right," Matt reluctantly agreed. He turned to face the old man. "Those matches are awfully valuable to us. We're not going to part with them cheaply. What are you offering?"

"How many matches are we talking about?"

Dani opened the box, took out five, which she

carefully wrapped in a plastic bag to protect from moisture, and then counted the rest. "Sixteen matches, plus we'll give you the box," she said.

The old man really wanted the matches. He'd had his eye on them from the moment they'd tumbled out of Dani's saddlebag, but he didn't want to appear eager. "I'll give you one sixteen-ounce can of creamed corn and the pack of Dentyne," he offered.

"You're kidding," Matt said.

"Take it or leave it," said Podlawski.

Matt looked at Dani. "What's your vote?" he asked.

"Leave it," she said.

"Same goes for me," agreed Matt. "No deal, Mr. Podlawski."

"Hmmmm." The old man pretended to think it over.

"Put the matches back in the saddlebag," Matt told Dani. "It doesn't look as if Mr. Podlawski wants to trade, after all."

"Hold on now. I didn't say that," said the old man a bit too quickly. He grimaced, knowing that he had shown more interest than he had intended, and he could tell from the look on their faces that they had caught him at it. "All right, how about the five-pound can of applesauce for the matches?"

"I don't know," said Dani. "Seems to me these matches can be pretty useful to a guy who lives in a dark basement. How about throwing in one sixty-four-ounce can of fruit cocktail, the can of creamed corn, two bottles of Yoo-Hoo, and the pack of gum?"

"That's almost as much as I was offering for the

whole horse!" he complained. "You're just giving me a lousy sixteen matches."

"You were offering too little for Herbie in the first place," said Matt with a smile. "That's our deal." And then he grinned. "Take it or leave it."

Sarge Podlawski took a deep breath and then slowly exhaled. These two weren't stupid. "I've been horn-swoggled by a couple of kids. All right. You've got a deal. But there's one hitch."

Matt and Dani eyed the old man suspiciously. "What is it?" asked Matt.

"When you finish eating this stuff, you promise to bury the cans and bottles. I don't want anybody finding that stuff nearby and figuring to look around the truck stop to see where it came from."

"Fair enough," said Matt. "You've got our word."

"Too bad you won't trade that horse." Podlawski sighed. "It's been longer than I can remember since I had a steak."

Herbie snorted.

The day turned surprisingly warm. It was nearly sixty degrees according to the thermometer Sarge Podlawski produced out of his basement home. "It's the warmest day since the war," he said. Then he peered out the truck stop's dining room window at the cloudy sky and added, "Maybe the brightest day, too. Could be the clouds are thinning out a bit."

It was welcome news if it was true.

"We'll be leaving when the hailstones are all melted," said Matt.

31

"At this rate," suggested Podlawski, "you'll be able to hit the road by tomorrow morning. I'll come up and see you off. Just bang on the pipes when it's time."

"You're really going to stay here all alone?" asked Dani.

"Wouldn't have it any other way. I do just fine by myself. I don't really need people—just their matches." He chuckled.

"But the more we help each other, the better our chances of survival," said Dani.

"That's probably true," agreed Podlawski. "I just wish I cared. I don't mean any harm to anyone, and I hope no one means any harm to me. But I'm just going to eat up my food in peace and quiet and leave the future to kids like you."

It was colder the next morning, but still in the low fifties. The hailstones were gone. Matt and Dani banged on the pipes, and the old man climbed up from his basement lair to offer his good-byes.

He had a surprise for them. Podlawski carried two bottles of Yoo-Hoo and an orange soda.

"You gave us our two bottles of Yoo-Hoo yesterday," Matt said.

"I know. I ain't senile yet," the old man replied with a laugh. "The honest truth is, I can't eat milk products—bad for my stomach—so I figured I'd give you another two bottles and we'd have ourselves a farewell toast."

They opened the two chocolate drinks and the

orange soda. Podlawski raised his bottle and said, "To good trades, good people, and a good future."

They clinked bottles and drank.

Matt and Dani barely knew the man, but it was still hard to say good-bye. They would always remember him as the Phantom of the Truck Stop. It was his choice to remain in that lonely place.

It was their choice to move on.

Chapter 6

IMAGINE," SAID DANI AS THE TRUCK STOP FADED FROM view behind them. "Denver is only one hundred miles from here. Isn't that what Sarge said?"

"Yeah. I wonder, how much of it is still standing?" Matt asked softly, not expecting an answer.

Dani gave him one, anyway. "If we're only one hundred miles away, and the truck stop is still standing, maybe Denver wasn't that badly hit. You saw how bad the damage was more than a hundred miles outside of St. Louis."

Matt nodded. She had a point. Usually everything around the big cities for a hundred miles or more had been turned to ash. As a rule, whenever they started seeing that kind of devastation, they circled around it, afraid of radiation poisoning.

"The easiest traveling is along the highway," said Matt. "So I guess we'll keep heading toward Denver and see what we find."

They rode on in silence for a while, enjoying the

surprising warmth they felt from the sun. It seemed as if the temperature would get up to sixty again. Although it was a good twenty degrees cooler than it used to be at that time of the year, Matt and Dani were grateful for the heat.

In the early afternoon, though, Matt spotted what looked like heavy clouds on the western horizon. "I knew this weather was too good to last," he muttered.

Dani saw the smudge of darkness low in the western sky and frowned. "I hope it's not another storm," she said wearily.

"If it is, it's pretty far away," said Matt. "Might as well forget about it now and take a break."

"Lunch?"

"You said the magic word."

They stopped and opened the five-pound can of applesauce, eating a little less than half of it. Having so much food was a luxury they hadn't experienced in the last few weeks. Despite their best intentions, they had opened the sixty-four-ounce can of fruit cocktail back at the truck stop. There was still a good fifty ounces left, but they had thoroughly devoured all of the creamed corn. It was startling how fast the food was disappearing without really satisfying their hunger.

Still, it was better than eating roots. But at the rate they were going, they'd be foraging for food again all too soon.

Back in the saddle after lunch, they noticed that the

dark cloud on the horizon hadn't moved. It was strange.

Later that afternoon the cloud still hadn't moved, although it did appear slightly larger. They tried not to pay any attention to it. As long as it was far away, the cloud wasn't an immediate threat. In any event, their attention was fixed on their fast-disappearing food.

"Maybe we ought to skip dinner," suggested Dani, as they made their evening camp at the side of the highway. "Let's try to make this stuff last a little longer."

"I can hold out if you can," said Matt.

"Deal."

Matt and Dani had lost count of the times they had gone to sleep hungry. It had become a way of life.

Before they drifted off to sleep, Matt said, "Did your mother ever tell you to eat all your food because there were people starving in Africa?"

"My mother used India."

"Do you think African and Indian mothers are telling their kids to clean their plates because there are children starving in America?" he asked.

"I hope so," Dani answered. "At least that would mean that people are alive in those places."

In the thoughtful silence that followed, Matt and Dani eventually fell asleep.

"Oh, no!" Dani cried when she woke up.

"What is it? What's wrong?" Matt asked breathlessly, awakened out of a dream in which he was just about to find his family.

"The food," she moaned. "One of the horses got into the saddlebags and licked both cans clean!"

Herbie had a guilty look on his face—not to mention applesauce on the top of his nose where his tongue couldn't reach. "And we saved your life," Matt yelled at his horse. "You call that gratitude?"

Whisk trotted up next to Herbie as if he planned to defend his friend.

"What do you want?" Matt demanded of Dani's horse.

Whisk ignored him and licked the applesauce off Herbie's nose.

Matt was so stunned by it all that he just helplessly slumped to the ground, defeated.

Dani was crying.

Furiously, Matt began to dig at the ground with his knife. He hacked away, making grunting sounds every time he stuck the blade into the earth.

Watching him, Dani got really scared. It seemed as if Matt had snapped.

"What are you doing?" she asked tentatively, putting her hand on his shoulder.

"Digging a hole for the cans, like we promised Sarge," he said gruffly. "Though, the way I see it, Herbie ought to be doing this instead of me."

Dani let out a deep sigh of relief. It was easier to deal with losing the food than losing Matt to madness. Either one of them could go over the edge at any time; it was something she thought about often. Sometimes she wondered how she was able to stay sane in this insane world. But she did. And she thought that Matt had something to do with it.

"It's our own fault," Matt said sourly as he put the empty cans in the deep hole he had dug. "We should have buckled the saddlebags so they couldn't get into them."

Trying to put the best face on their disaster, Dani reluctantly agreed. "Can't blame them," she said, resigned. "They're hungry, too."

"Well, at least Herbie didn't drink the Yoo-Hoo," Matt joked halfheartedly.

"Just don't give him a bottle opener for Christmas."

They laughed weakly and got to their feet.

Dani did a double take when she looked at the western horizon. "Hey," she said, surprise in her voice. "That cloud out there isn't a cloud at all."

The air was surprisingly clear, and as Matt stared, a smile slowly formed on his lips. "You're right," he said. "Those aren't clouds. They're the Rocky Mountains. We're getting there, Dani!" he exclaimed happily, all thoughts of the food disaster forgotten. "California is on the other side of those mountains. We're going to make it, Dani. I feel it. I know it. We're going to make it!"

Chapter 7

MATT AND DANI RODE ALL MORNING TOWARD THE mountains but never seemed to get any closer. They didn't stop—as they usually did—in the early afternoon to rest. The Rockies beckoned them on. They kept riding, pushing themselves and their horses, trying to reach the mountains, a great milestone in their trek across America.

At midafternoon they finally did have to stop to rest their horses. After removing their saddles, Matt and Dani dried and brushed their mounts, letting them roll and graze in the short grass nearby.

"I hate to admit it," Dani said, "but I'm hungry."

"Have a piece of gum," Matt suggested, offering her a piece of Dentyne.

"I hate to waste it."

"Well, you can always leave it on your bedpost overnight," he replied, singing the last few words of an old comedy song.

"Yeah. If I only had a bedpost—not to mention a bed."

She took the gum and savored its flavor. "I never liked Dentyne," she admitted. "But it sure tastes good now."

Matt popped a piece of Dentyne in his mouth, too. As he reverently chewed the cinnamon-flavored gum, he said, "As hungry as I am, I'd chow down on tuna ice cream."

All the time they were talking, neither Matt nor Dani took their eyes off the Rocky Mountains. They were still so distant. Were they a day and a half away? Two days? Three days?

"Come on, let's get going," Matt said impatiently. "The horses have had enough rest. Besides, we can maybe get another five miles closer before sundown."

"That's okay by me," Dani said. "But we'd better look around for something to eat before we go, because it'll get too dark to forage later."

There were a few stunted trees near a dry creekbed. While Dani collected dead wood for the fire they'd build later on, Matt made a quick search of the surviving plants, pulling the first three out of the ground that seemed as if they might have edible roots. He cut off the roots and threw them into his saddlebag. "We'll boil these later," he announced. "Let's go."

They quickly saddled up and drove their horses on until the blurred image of the sun, trapped behind the deep magenta clouds, began sinking below the rim of the distant mountains.

* * *

"Good fire," Matt said approvingly, gazing into the yellow flames Dani had created.

"Used just one match," she said proudly.

The roots sat in their aluminum pot, which was half filled with boiling water.

"Just like mother used to make," Matt said, kidding. He shoved the roots around in the water with his knife.

Dani stuck her well-chewed piece of gum on the edge of her tin plate. "I'm going to need this to kill the taste of the roots."

"Maybe we ought to wash this crud down with our Yoo-Hoo," Matt suggested.

Dani shook her head, then smiled in the firelight. "Let's save it for when we reach the Rockies. It'll be a celebration."

"Yeah," Matt said quietly, staring off into the dark night toward the unseen mountains.

They put off eating for as long as they could. The roots were anything but appetizing. Finally, though, their hunger overcame their reluctance and they began eating the bitter-tasting food.

Dani ate one of the roots and stopped. "If these had been part of my regular diet at home," she stated, "I wouldn't have ever had any trouble with my weight. We've eaten tree bark that tasted better. This gets my vote for the absolute worst meal we've ever had. I don't even know what it was. Do you?"

"Don't remember the name, but I'm sure we've had it before. It does taste a little funny, though, doesn't it?" he asked while chewing his second root.

" 'Funny' isn't the word." Dani made a face. "Maybe you'd better stop. We should have had just a taste of it and then waited four hours to see if it was safe."

Just as she finished speaking, Matt swallowed the second root.

"Why didn't you spit it out?"

"I'd already gone through the worst of it—chewing that awful stuff," he said. "It seemed like such a waste to suffer without the payoff."

She laughed in spite of herself.

"Instead of worrying about the food," he said, "you ought to keep an eye on the fire. It's going out."

They quickly added what little wood they had left to the embers, and the flames leapt back to life, widening their island of light for a short while longer before the darkness reclaimed the land. But by then, Matt and Dani had rolled out their blankets and had gone to sleep.

It was the middle of the night when Matt woke up—he was in a cold sweat. His head felt as if someone were drilling inside his brain. The pain was excruciating. And he couldn't believe how nauseated he was. His stomach was on some sort of internal roller coaster.

The first thing he realized was that the roots they had eaten were contaminated. The second thing he realized was that he was going to throw up.

He lurched over on to his side and threw up most of

44

the roots. It didn't help. His stomach was still roiling, and his head was pounding like a jackhammer.

Weakly, Matt scraped up some dirt and covered his vomit. Then he lay back down and closed his eyes, hoping to sleep so he could wake up feeling better.

A few minutes later, almost as if it were in a dream, Matt heard a moaning sound. It was Dani.

"You awake?" he panted breathlessly, wanting to tell her he was ill.

His answer came as she retched and threw up just as he had done.

"We poisoned ourselves," Dani whispered with great effort as she slumped back down on her blanket.

"We'll be all right in the morning," Matt offered hopefully. "It's probably good that we threw up. It cleaned us out."

Except Matt continued to retch all night. Even though nothing came up out of his stomach, the nausea wouldn't go away. Nor would the headache. He started to shiver uncontrollably.

Dani was luckier. Just as Matt had suggested, she did begin to feel better in the morning; at least she was in better shape than Matt. But then he had eaten more of the roots than she had.

"You look terrible," Dani said with deep concern in her voice. "Do you think you can travel?"

"I'll be sick no matter where I am," Matt replied bravely. "I might as well be heading west."

Dani saddled both of the horses and cleaned up the camp while Matt lay quietly on the ground, trying to conserve his energy. When it was time to climb up on Herbie, Matt struggled to his feet as a wave of dizziness sent him reeling. He fell over and retched again, his stomach and throat raw from his sickness. "The poison's in my bloodstream," he said softly. "There's nothing left in my belly."

Dani tenderly leaned down over him and kissed his forehead. Her lips lingered there a moment. "You've got a fever," she announced.

Matt smiled crookedly. "My mother used to do that."

"Mine, too."

"You can take my temperature anytime," he said, trying to banter so she wouldn't know how sick he really was.

Leaning on Dani, Matt stood and slowly climbed up into the saddle.

"Don't worry, I'll get better," he promised.

But he didn't. In fact, he got much worse.

Chapter 8

Sweat poured down Matt's face and his shirt clung to him. The whole time he was riding, the Rocky Mountains floated before him like a mirage. Sometimes they loomed large in his mind's eye, at other times they seemed impossibly far away.

"How are you doing?" Dani asked anxiously, glancing back at him over her shoulder.

Matt nodded, but she could see he was suffering. For that matter, she wasn't feeling too well herself, but she knew she was over the worst of her own illness.

A short while later they stopped for a rest.

"Here," Dani said, handing him a plastic water bottle. "Have something to drink."

He swallowed two mouthfuls and immediately threw them up. "Can't hold anything in my stomach," he said.

Dani was worried. With his high fever, Matt might get seriously dehydrated if he couldn't replenish the water in his system.

"I want to make it to the mountains," Matt said.

The words came out in a weak whisper that almost sounded like a last wish. He raised his head defiantly, though, and insisted, "I know I'll feel better when we get there. Let's go."

They continued on. And finally, the Rockies really did begin to take shape. They were no longer a dark cloud on the horizon. Dani could make out the rusty color of the brownish-red foothills, the towering height of the entire chain, and the magnificent, snow-capped, jagged peaks. She was befuddled, though, by the sight of something small and dark near the foot of the mountain range. At first, she couldn't figure out what it was. Then she sighted along the highway and saw that the road seemed to lead right into it. Her eyes lit up with excitement.

"Matt!" she cried, turning in her saddle. "It's Denver! Look!"

All she saw, however, was Herbie and an empty saddle. Matt had passed out and fallen off the horse a hundred yards back. He was lying on the side of the road, unconscious.

The tumble to the ground hadn't hurt Matt, but the poison inside his body was killing him. Dani was shocked at how hot his skin felt; his temperature was clearly soaring. She doused his face with cold water from her canteen to cool him off and, she hoped, to wake him up.

Matt's eyes fluttered open and he said, "Did we reach the Rockies yet?"

"Almost," said Dani tenderly. "How do you feel?"

48

Matt shook his head and closed his eyes.

"Don't go to sleep," she pleaded. "There's a city just down the road—Denver. There might be people there; somebody to help you," she said, though she didn't really believe it. She had seen no sign of life up ahead, but she wanted Matt to have hope. "You've got to keep going," she said, shaking him. "Do you hear me?"

Matt didn't answer.

She tried to help him up, but he was out cold. Matt was one hundred and thirty pounds of dead weight. All she could do was make him comfortable and hope he'd come to.

As the hours dragged on, Dani mopped his head with a cold, damp cloth, wondering what would become of her if he should die out there on the high plains. But every time that thought entered her mind, Dani hated herself for her selfishness. She knew it was Matt that she should be worried about, not herself. But she couldn't help it. She was scared for him, and scared for herself.

Matt was deathly pale, he was sweating and shivering at the same time, and his lips were so dry they were beginning to crack. Even more frightening to her was that Matt was becoming delirious; he'd mumble something incoherent, then start crying, and just as suddenly begin shouting, only to collapse into tears again. But he wouldn't wake up.

Dani was afraid he'd never wake up. She felt as if she were sitting there waiting for him to die.

And she couldn't stand it.

Her inability to help him was driving her crazy. Even her attempts at making him drink only resulted in water dribbling down his chin. She wanted desperately to save him, only she didn't know how.

As the sun set over the Rockies, Dani built a fire out of kindling from nearby dead bushes. Matt instinctively rolled toward the fire for its warmth. Seeing that he was cold, she wrapped her own blanket around him and caressed his hair.

"Please get well," she murmured. "You're the best friend I've got." She laughed darkly to herself. "You're the *only* friend I've got."

There was no more wood to throw on the fire, and it slowly died, the flames retreating to a red glow that lasted a surprisingly long time before the dark night won its final victory.

Dani was afraid that Matt might need her, so she tried to stay awake. She held him close, letting his head rest in her lap, feeling his raspy, difficult breathing as his chest rose and fell.

She was used to black nights and therefore didn't expect to see anything. And that was why she was shocked when dozens of little dancing lights caught her eye.

I wonder what they are? she thought. *They can't be stars.* She carefully shifted her position so as not to disturb Matt, but she absently put her hand down in the cold campfire and felt the ashes crumble at her touch. "That's what they are," she suddenly blurted out loud while rubbing her hand clean. "Campfires!" Those flickering lights had to be coming from

50

Denver, she reasoned. There *were* people there—and maybe they'd help Matt. It was his only hope.

The distant lights sparkled in Dani's dreams as she finally fell asleep. When she awoke at dawn, she was no longer sure if she had really seen the campfires or if she had merely dreamt them.

There was only one way to find out.

"Matt? Can you hear me?" Dani said, shaking him gently.

He groaned but didn't wake up.

She shook him again; it didn't do any good.

Dani glanced to the west and saw what she believed was the city of Denver off in the distance. She kissed Matt's forehead, and his temperature filled her with dread. He clearly wasn't getting any better. If anything, he was probably worse. She had to get help for him—and soon. But there was no way on earth that she could hoist him onto Herbie all by herself. In other words, he wasn't going anywhere.

It was time to make a hard decision.

The thought of leaving Matt behind while she rode off to look for help made her uneasy. What if a wild animal attacked him? What if he woke up while she was away and thought that she had abandoned him? Or worst of all, what if she didn't return in time and Matt died all alone?

Dani was tortured by her fears, but she also knew that to do nothing would condemn Matt to certain death. In the end, she decided, she had no choice.

Dani left everything that Matt would need within

51

easy reach should he wake up before her return. For herself, Dani took only one canteen, which she slung over her shoulder. Matt had the saddlebags, as well as a full canteen, two plastic water bottles, the tiny bit of food left from Sarge Podlawski, and all of their weapons except for the knife that Dani wore in a scabbard on her belt.

As sick as Matt was, Dani knew that there was little time to spare. She decided to take both horses so that she could travel as quickly as possible, riding one horse until it tired, then switching to the other. For Matt's sake, however, she took only one saddle and saddle blanket, figuring to change saddles whenever she changed horses. In that way, Dani could snugly wrap Matt in the second blanket.

It was time to go.

Matt was moaning in his sleep and sweating as if it were a tropical summer day. Dani knelt down beside him and stroked his sweat-drenched hair. "Somehow, I'll find help," she said. "I'll race the whole way, and I'll get back as soon as I can. I promise." And then in a whisper she added, "Please, Matt—don't die."

Chapter 9

ALTHOUGH MATT DIDN'T OPEN HIS EYES, HE SENSED Dani's hand brushing through his hair. More than that, he heard her voice. It sounded far away, as if she were calling to him across a storm-tossed beach. The words she spoke were lost in the pounding surf, which was really his pounding heartbeat. He strained to hear what she was saying.

It seemed as if she was trying to tell him something important—something about a "race." That was all he could make out, yet in his delirium he felt he understood. They had been racing ever since they fled their hometown of Fair Oaks, racing from scavengers, dust storms, and clouds of insects.

Dani's hand lifted from his head, and he missed her gentle touch. He wanted to reach out to her, but he couldn't lift his arms. He knew there was another race to be run—Dani had said so—but he was unable to move, and it scared him.

The clatter of horses' hooves reached Matt's ears.

Had the race already begun? He was so tired. Why did he have to keep running? Who was after him? Matt moaned, his mind drifting into a web of dark memories. . . .

It was track-and-field day, and he was representing his eighth-grade class in the cross-country race. It was the last event of the games. His class needed one more point to come in first. That meant he only needed a third-place finish. There were nine other kids running, and every one of them was faster than he was.

The gun sounded and he took off with the pack. He stayed near the leaders as they circled the athletic field and followed the path up the hill through the woods and along the river.

It seemed incredible, but he was in third place at the halfway point and he felt terrific. Keith Brinkerhoff was trailing him in fourth place, but he didn't seem to be a threat.

Brinkerhoff. He was a tall, muscular kid with a shock of blond hair. Played the drums. The girls just loved him. He even had a dimple. What a thrill it was going to be to beat him.

Matt kept a steady pace, stayed ahead of Brinkerhoff, and emerged third from the woods to circle the houses near the school parking lot. He passed the tennis courts and headed for the turn around the far end of the school.

But now his lungs were burning. His legs were heavy. Every step was pure agony, but he struggled on.

He turned the corner, and there it was—the long straightaway of five hundred yards to the finish line. It seemed as if the entire school were there, waiting to see who the victors would be.

He looked over his shoulder. Keith Brinkerhoff had just gone into his kick and was gaining on him. How could Brinkerhoff have anything left after such a long run? Matt had to think, use strategy, break Brinkerhoff's will. There had to be a way to save his third-place finish.

There was just one chance. Pacing himself, he waited until Brinkerhoff came up beside him, then he smiled broadly at his opponent and used every ounce of reserve energy to jump into a sprint.

He pulled away. When Brinkerhoff saw him race ahead, the challenger simply threw up his hands and gave up.

Matt had nothing left, but Brinkerhoff didn't know it. He had faked his opponent out and the third-place ribbon was going to be his. He could see his cheering classmates, hear their shouts of encouragement.

And then he went down!

His right leg spasmed and he collapsed. Clutching at his thigh, he cried out in pain. Brinkerhoff didn't stop to help him. He crossed the finish line just fifty yards away and took third place.

As the sun moved across the Colorado sky, Matt relived that same agonizing moment over and over. Unconscious, he tossed and turned in his blanket, unaware that he was in yet another race—this one for his life. But ironically, the two races were not so dissimilar; in both of them he was falling short of the finish line.

Dani continued galloping west on the high plains, following Interstate 70 toward the Rocky Mountains and the city that sat at its feet. She had already ridden Whisk, switched to Herbie, and then back again to Whisk. It was midafternoon, and she had traveled hard since the early morning.

Somewhere behind her, Matt was lying on the ground, sick, alone, and unprotected. Dani never forgot it. She pushed herself and the horses to the breaking point, trying to reach Denver before nightfall.

At first her goal seemed impossible, but as the day wore on, the tall buildings of the city began to come clear in the hazy sunshine. Soon, she was passing small clusters of houses at the outskirts of the city. Then she raced through what had once been Denver's suburbs.

Dani saw the broken windows and smashed doors of the suburban houses. The streets were littered with cars stripped of anything useful. Dani assumed that the houses she passed had been ransacked as well. But now there were no looters; the streets were quiet and empty except for the hoofbeats of her own horses.

The dark outlines of the city skyline up ahead reminded her of dinosaur skeletons in a museum. Both were relics of the past. Dani hadn't seen the skyscrapers of a city since before the night of the war.

As far as she knew, every great city in the country had been leveled by nuclear missiles. Yet somehow Denver had been spared.

Or had it?

The damage Dani saw was all man-made, and that made her wonder what had happened to all the people. If there was no one there, then who had lit the fires she had seen the night before?

Or had those dancing lights been in a dream?

Dani refused to believe that such a large city with its great, tall buildings could be totally deserted. Yet so far she hadn't seen anyone—alive or dead.

She switched horses again, riding Herbie for the last leg of her journey. Dani didn't know what she would do if Denver was truly empty of all life.

The sun began to fall behind the mountains and Dani rode on in deepening shadows. She traveled across a huge airport called Stapleton International, passed signs for the Rocky Mountain Arsenal, and kept on going. Most of the street signs were still standing, and she followed them, making a left turn off the interstate onto Colorado Boulevard. She was heading for downtown Denver.

That's when she saw smoke rising between two skyscrapers. Tears flowed freely down her face. She wanted to shout with joy, because smoke meant not only fire but also people. She prayed that Matt could hold out long enough for her to return with help.

"Come on," she urged Herbie. "I know you're beat. So am I. But we've got to do this for Matt."

The animal's ear pricked up at the mention of its

master's name. It struggled to gallop, heading toward the smell of wood smoke—and the smell of food.

Dani continued down the broad lanes of Colorado Boulevard and then made a right turn on East Colfax Avenue. The tall buildings were straight ahead. She passed signs for hospitals, colleges, parks, and botanical gardens.

She followed East Colfax until the street came to an abrupt end, blocked by a string of rusting cars and trucks. Dani rode up to it and searched for a narrow gap through which she could pass and continue her journey. It was getting dark and she had to find help soon.

There was a space at the edge of the avenue between the wall of a building and an overturned Cadillac. "Come on," she said, pointing Herbie into the gap. But the horse hesitated and snorted.

"What is it? What's wrong?" Dani asked nervously, looking around for whatever had spooked Herbie.

She found her answer as six men with knives, hatchets, and axes, suddenly emerged from their hiding place.

_____ Chapter 10 _____

THE MEN MOVED QUICKLY—TOO QUICKLY FOR DANI TO react. One of them grabbed the rope tethering Whisk to Herbie. A second man snatched Herbie's reins out of Dani's hands. Shocked by the suddenness of their actions and knowing there was nowhere to run, Dani sat atop Herbie, frozen like a deer caught in the headlights of an oncoming car.

"Get down off that horse," ordered a big, lumbering man with a heavy black beard.

"I—I don't think I will," Dani replied nervously, looking at the rough-looking men who stared up at her.

The man with the beard reached up, took Dani by the arm, and hauled her out of the saddle. Before her feet hit the street, the man deftly plucked the knife from its scabbard on her belt.

"Tie her hands," the bearded man ordered someone standing behind her. Dani's arms were pulled behind her back and she felt a coarse piece of rope.

tighten around her wrists. She looked over her shoulder and saw a tall, thin young man of perhaps nineteen or twenty staring back at her with troubled blue eyes.

"Why are you doing this?" she asked him.

The young man took a deep breath and said, "It's our job to protect the city. We don't know who you are, and—"

"Wait!" Dani cut him off, crying out with relief and happiness. "You're not bandits? Scavengers?"

The young man squinted at her with a thoughtful look on his face. "Hardly," he said.

"Then you're exactly who I'm looking for!" she declared.

"Finish tying her up," ordered the bearded man, ignoring Dani.

"You don't understand," she said. "I saw your campfires last night and thought there might be people here. I need help. I left my friend out on the plains. He's sick and needs a doctor, medicine. It's some kind of food poisoning. Please. I've been riding since dawn to get here."

"Put a gag on her," said the bearded man.

"You know, she could be telling the truth," suggested the young man who was knotting the rope around Dani's wrists.

"Yeah, and maybe the Broncos are going to win the Super Bowl this year," replied the bearded man sarcastically.

A piece of cloth was suddenly slipped over Dani's face and pulled tight across her mouth.

She couldn't believe it. She had come all that way looking for help, had found who she was looking for, *and they wouldn't listen to her!*

"What are we going to do with her, Chet?" one of the men asked their bearded leader.

"Best thing is probably to cut her throat and leave the body here for her slave-trading biker friends to find," he replied. "That ought to teach them to stay clear of Denver."

Dani's eyes opened wide in horror.

"Don't like that, do you, girlie?" sneered the man named Chet. "Thought if you came on horseback we wouldn't suspect you. Even brought a second horse along to carry one of our kids away, huh?"

Tears formed in Dani's eyes. Everything was going wrong.

The young man who had tied Dani's hands looked at her and then cleared his throat. "You know," he said, "we might be handling this the wrong way."

"What do you mean?" asked Chet suspiciously.

"Well, let's assume for the sake of argument that she's really tied up with those slave traders," he replied. "We could get this girl to lead us to them. And with a fully armed Denver Defense Squad, we could wipe them out once and for all. It's just like you always say, Chet, 'the best defense is a good offense.' All we've got to do is convince the council to go along with the plan. What do you say?"

"Brian's got a good idea," said the man holding Whisk's reins.

"Yeah," agreed yet another man in the group. "If

the council will go along with it, we can wipe the scum right off the face of the earth."

"Brian," the leader said as he put a hand on the young man's broad shoulders, "you're taking after your mother. Yep. You're getting to be a regular politician."

"I think I've just been insulted," said Brian good-naturedly.

"Hey, I like your mother," countered Chet. "I just wish she'd stick to doctoring. Anyway, let's take the girl to the council to see what they want to do with her."

As they marched past the wall of rusted cars and trucks, Dani caught Brian's eye and tried to indicate how grateful she was. No matter what his motives, he had given her another chance to save Matt.

He flashed a quick warm smile at her.

For some reason that Dani couldn't fathom, she blushed.

Matt shivered in his sleep. The blanket that Dani had wrapped around him had fallen away because of his violent thrashing.

The cold revived him and forced him to open his eyes. He was lying on his back, looking up at what should have been the sky. But there was nothing but an impenetrable blackness above him. It was almost as if his eyes had never really opened.

"Dani?" he croaked through parched lips.

No answer.

"Dani?" he weakly rasped again.

Silence.

His head was spinning, and he felt pain in every joint and muscle in his body. But what hurt most was that Dani wasn't there.

He moved his right arm, and his hand struck something familiar. From touch he knew it was a plastic water bottle. He had precious little strength, but he had to have that water.

Clasping the bottle, he pulled it toward him and slowly, painfully twisted the cap off the top. Rising up on his elbows, he nearly passed out twice, but he fought the darkness inside of himself and struggled to stay awake.

When the bottle was finally open, he lifted it to his lips and took a small mouthful of cold water. He would have liked more, but a wave of dizziness washed over him. He fell back to the ground and passed out, the bottle slipping from his hands and the water spilling out onto the earth.

This time there were no dreams of a race. There were no dreams at all. He was unconscious, unaware of the bitterly cold night, his thirst, his pain, and his life slowly ebbing away. . . .

_____ Chapter 11 _____

DANI LOOKED UP AT THE ROTUNDA OF THE COLORADO State Capitol on East Colfax Avenue. Denver's survivors used the grand old building to house their fledgling democracy. One of Dani's captors had been sent ahead, so the leaders of that society were already gathered inside.

Chet, Brian, and the three other Denver Defense Squad members followed Dani into what had once been the State Senate Chamber. The huge hall was lit by torchlight, and about forty of the seats were filled with elected representatives of the remnants of this once great city.

After removing Dani's gag and the rope binding her wrists, Chet gave his report, telling the council where and how they had captured this female intruder.

Dani was so stunned by the sight of so many people in one place that she could hardly pay attention. She kept looking at the council members and the packed visitors' gallery on the second floor. People were shouting, but to Dani it was a wonderful symphony of life.

All at once the tall, young man named Brian gave her a gentle nudge in the side.

"What is it?" she asked.

"The mayor asked you a question," he whispered.

"Oh," she said, not quite sure whom to turn to. "What was the question?"

"I asked," repeated a bald, middle-aged man with a pair of cracked glasses, "how many slave traders are there in your group?"

"None."

"Well, it seems we've already caught you in a lie," the mayor said with disgust. "According to Chet, you told him in front of five other witnesses that you had an accomplice out on the high plains."

"A friend, not an accomplice," insisted Dani. "But he's not a slave trader, and neither am I. Look," she said a little desperately, "I came here for help. I need a doctor or some medicine. My friend ate some roots that made him very sick. Help is all I want, all I need. My friend doesn't have much time. Won't you please help me?"

Dani might just as well have been talking to Herbie.

The mayor turned and whispered to an adviser sitting on his right. He nodded once and continued his questioning. "Where did you and your friend come from?" he asked.

"Fair Oaks, New Jersey. We're trying to get to California."

The people in the hall started buzzing, talking to one another excitedly. The mayor had to rap his gavel half a dozen times to restore order in the chamber.

"My dear young lady," said the mayor. "You don't really expect us to believe that you've waltzed across two thousand miles of a nuclear-devastated wasteland, do you?"

"I don't care if you believe it or not," Dani shot back. "It just happens to be the truth. Let me tell you, it wasn't easy getting this far. And if you don't help me, my friend isn't going to get any farther."

During this time Brian had been conferring with a short, plump woman who looked about fifty years old. She stood up now and waved her hand.

"Yes, Dr. Stoddard, what is it?"

The woman lowered her hand, glanced at Brian, and smiled. Then she cleared her throat and said, "It seems to me that this girl's story is so farfetched that it's probably true. Any self-respecting outlaw would have made up a much more credible tale. My son, Brian, was there when the girl was caught, and he tells me that as soon as she learned that she had been captured by the Denver Defense Squad, she was thrilled. That's hardly the reaction of a slave trader, now, is it?"

"So what are you suggesting, Dr. Stoddard?" asked one of the council members.

"That at first light tomorrow we send a large contingent of well-armed citizens out with this girl to find her friend. If it's a trap, she'll be the first to die. In any event, there'll be a sufficient number of us to fight off any band of bikers. I'll travel with the group to attend to the sick young man."

There was a roar of protest from the council and the gallery. The mayor gaveled them quiet again. He spoke for the majority when he said, "We can't afford to send a doctor out of the city. There are only six doctors left in all of Denver, and we can't risk that you'll be killed or captured. I'm sorry, Dr. Stoddard, but your suggestion is out of the question."

"Mr. Mayor!" called out Brian Stoddard.

Dani turned to look at him, wondering what he would say.

"Go ahead, Brian," said the mayor.

"Well, I'm no doctor, but I have been studying a bit with my mother. She could give me the medicine, and I could travel out of the city in her place."

A member of the council jumped to his feet and angrily shouted, "Why are we wasting our time on this matter? Even if this girl is telling the truth, what difference does it make if her friend lives or dies? I don't mean to sound hard-hearted, but untold millions of people have died. This girl is nothing to us. Her friend—even if he exists—means even less. Let's move on to the next order of business!"

The council and the gallery erupted into applause.

"No!" The room was shocked into silence by the vehemence of an aged council member, who slowly rose to his feet, pushing himself up against the desk in front of him. "If we don't help this young woman and her friend, then we're no better than the slave trad-ers," he declared. "I say, if we claim to be civilized, let's act like it!"

There was a combination of jeering and applause.

Dani turned sorrowful eyes on Brian Stoddard, hoping he would know what to say to sway the crowd to her side.

"Just a minute!" Brian declared. "We don't live in a vacuum. There's a whole country east of here that we know nothing about. The people who left Denver migrated into the southern Rockies. No one went east. We don't know what's really out there. But this girl and her friend do. If someday we're going to put the pieces of this country back together again, we need to know what happened to the land. These two people will be valuable resources."

The council and Denver's citizens argued on for hours. It was democracy the way it had been practiced two hundred years before with everyone having his or her say. In the end they voted that Brian Stoddard could leave the city with the captured girl under the following conditions: He would have no armed guard; he would travel unescorted, except for Dani; he would carry just enough medicine for one person; and if captured, he would not expect anyone from Denver to try to rescue him.

"Do you agree to the terms?" asked the mayor after the vote was taken.

Brian took Dani by the arm and forced her to face him. "I'm betting my life that you're telling the truth," he said. "I'd like to hear it one more time. Is there really someone out there who's sick and needs help?"

Dani looked him straight in the eye and said, "Yes."

But Brian didn't immediately accept the council's terms. He walked over to his mother and asked, "Do you think I'm making a mistake?"

"I believe her," said Dr. Stoddard simply. "But that doesn't mean I think it's safe out there. I don't think you should leave Denver alone."

"She's awfully pretty," said Brian.

At that, his mother laughed. "Well, at least you've got a good reason."

"There's another reason," Brian whispered. "I'd like to run for the council someday. This would be a good opportunity to show everybody what I'm made of."

"It's kind of grandstanding, isn't it?" his mother asked gently.

"Maybe." He shrugged. "But it'll get everyone's attention."

"Well, I raised you to make up your own mind, so do what you feel is right. Just be careful. And please come home safe and sound."

"I will, Mom. And thanks."

Brian walked back toward Dani and announced, "I accept the terms of the council." Then he turned to the grateful girl at his side and said, "You'd better get some sleep. You and I are leaving at sunup."

Chapter 12

LYING ON HIS STOMACH, THE RIGHT SIDE OF HIS FACE pressed against the cold ground, Matt stirred gently in the late-afternoon sun. The bugs crawling beneath his clothing took no notice of his movement; they were busy with their own survival.

Matt's fever was still high and he was riddled with chills. He was too sick to be hungry, but his thirst was so great that his tongue had swelled in his throat, nearly choking him. The urge to breathe, to drink, to live, made Matt struggle toward consciousness. But he couldn't quite get there. He could do no better than reach a sort of delirious stupor, in which his mind was a jumble of disconnected thoughts.

In this twilight state, Matt clawed at the hard-packed earth with his hands, thinking that he could dig a well to supply him with all the water he'd ever need. He managed to scrape three inches into the earth, then he suddenly stopped, afraid that he'd fall into the well and drown. He tried to roll away from the hole he had dug, imagining it a massive crater.

Although he could hardly move, his effort forced him to open his eyes. In a blurry focus, Matt thought he saw two bicycles rolling toward him in the distance. They seemed so unreal, so unexpected, that he knew he was dreaming. In that moment, he was sure that all of it—the well, the bicycles—were in his imagination. *Maybe everything is a dream: the war, the endless trek, Dani. . . .*

No, please, he thought as he drifted into unconsciousness again. *Don't let Dani be a dream.*

Dani pedaled a ten-speed bike, guiding it down the middle of Interstate 70 with Brian Stoddard and Herbie trailing behind. "We're getting close," she declared.

"That's the eighth time you've said that in the last five minutes," Stoddard complained. "I hate to say this, but I'm starting to have some serious doubts about you."

"I'm not lying," Dani insisted. "He's here somewhere. I just didn't realize how far I had ridden yesterday."

Brian Stoddard was sweating, but not from the bicycling. He was in a constant state of alert, his eyes darting warily, expecting to see hordes of slave traders rise up from every hidden hollow or gully.

It wasn't Dani who found Matt, it was Herbie. The horse whinnied at the familiar scent of its master.

Dani untied the rope that had tethered Herbie to her bike. The horse trotted ahead, found Matt, and stood licking his face.

Although her legs were aching from biking so long and far, Dani raced all the way to Matt. When she reached him, lying face down on the ground, she leapt off her bike and ran the last few steps to him, terrified that he was already dead.

Brian Stoddard was behind her.

Dani felt Matt's hot skin. "Thank God," she whispered. "It's not too late." Then she turned toward Brian and joyfully shouted, "He's alive! Hurry!"

Stoddard moved quickly, but carefully. It could still be a trap. The guy on the ground could be playing possum, waiting to leap up and kill him. Brian remained cautious. He approached the body warily, a machete in his right hand poised to strike in case Matt made any sudden moves.

"Come on, Stoddard," Dani said scornfully as she rolled Matt over onto his back. "Does this poor guy look like he's going to jump up and knife you?"

Brian got his first clear view of Matt, and he immediately knew that Dani was right. He sheathed his machete and rushed to Matt's side.

"Just looking at him," said Brian, "it's obvious that he's badly dehydrated. That's probably his worst problem right now."

"What can you do for him?" Dani asked plaintively.

Brian didn't answer. Instead, he took a cloth out of his backpack and soaked it with water. He held it over Matt's mouth and squeezed it, water falling like a light rain onto Matt's lips, dripping down into his mouth.

Matt coughed, but the liquid disappeared.

"He was spitting everything up before," Dani said. "How come he can swallow now?"

"He isn't really swallowing," explained Brian. "It's more like absorption. He's so dried out that his body is like a sponge, sucking up all available moisture."

Brian felt Matt's forehead. "He's burning up. He really needs this water." The doctor's son handed Dani the cloth and said, "Keep doing what I did. He needs as much water as possible, but give it to him gradually. Too much too soon will do more harm than good."

Dani did as she was told, dripping the water into Matt's mouth, while saying, "You're going to be all right. I brought help, just like I promised. Brian will take care of you. You'll see, you'll be as good as new in no time."

Brian watched Dani out of the corner of his eye as he went through his backpack to get the medicine his mother had given him. He had come to see this girl as a rough, hard-edged beauty, but now he observed a tenderness and sweetness about her that surprised him. Her combination of strength and gentleness was very appealing to Brian. He already knew he liked the way she looked.

They spent the rest of the afternoon giving Matt water and applying cold compresses to his forehead, trying to lower his temperature. Brian also gave Matt the first of a series of shots to fight against the food poisoning and fever. He stuck the syringe in Matt's

74

buttocks and then all they could do was hope for the best.

Before night fell Dani gathered dead wood from nearby bushes to build a fire.

"Better not," said Brian.

"Think I'm signaling my slave-trader friends?" she challenged.

"No," he conceded. "But there's no point in drawing any strangers to us."

"But Matt needs the warmth," said Dani. "We ought to have a fire for him."

"I'll give up my blanket," Brian offered.

Dani smiled at Brian in the fading light. "That's very nice of you. You don't even know Matt."

"I'm not doing it for him," said Brian. "I'm doing it for you."

"Oh." Dani didn't know what else to say.

Dani and Brian took turns caring for Matt through the night. It seemed as if the darkness would never end. And it seemed as if Matt would not get better. But about an hour before dawn, Brian heard Matt sigh deeply, as if he were letting go of something deep within himself.

He felt Matt's forehead. It was no longer hot. The worst was finally over. Or perhaps, he thought, it was just beginning. . . .

In the deep charcoal light of the false dawn, Brian stared down at Matt and wondered what this young man and Dani had in common. She obviously cared about him. But how much? And in what way?

Brian wanted the answers to those questions.

What he didn't know was that Matt had been wanting the answers to those very questions himself.

Even though she was worn out, Dani woke up at dawn out of long-standing habit. "How is he?" were the first words she spoke.

"Fever broke," Brian announced with a grin.

"I can't believe it!" she cried happily, reaching out to hug Brian. "You really did it!"

"Nah," said Brian modestly. "It wasn't me. It was the water, the cold compresses, and the medicine. Or maybe the fever would have broken, anyway. Who knows? Anyway, I'll give him another shot before we leave."

Dani hurried to Matt's side and saw the peaceful look on his face. There were tears in her eyes when she turned back to face Brian. "No, it wasn't any of those things," she said, giving him her warmest smile. "It was because you trusted me. And you weren't willing to let Matt die. I'll always be grateful to you. And so will Matt, when he finally wakes up."

"Well, he's not out of the woods yet," said Brian. "He needs plenty of food and rest. There's only so much we can do for him here, so we ought to get him back to Denver. The sooner the better."

After Matt had another shot, Brian and Dani picked him up and laid him over Herbie's back. They tied him down and slowly headed back toward Denver. At the pace they had to travel—with frequent stops to tend to him—they knew it would take more than twice as long to return to the city.

As they rode their bikes back along the cracked and broken interstate, Dani and Brian talked about all sorts of things. As the day wore on, she told him about her life before the war, her travels since, and her absolute delight—beyond what it meant for Matt—at finding an actual city full of people who had survived the war.

Brian had to laugh. "It isn't much of a city," he said. "There are only about six hundred of us left— you saw a lot of us the other night at the council meeting."

"But you weren't hit by the missiles?" countered Dani.

"No, we weren't hit by the missiles," he conceded. "The best anyone can figure—because no one wants to go and actually look—is that the missiles struck north of us, up in the Rockies. I can tell you this much, firestorms lit the sky for nearly a month after the war, burning everything in the mountains above the city."

The sun was setting behind the Rockies, but in the fading light she could see how bare the mountains were. There were only snowcapped peaks with nothing green showing below the frost line.

"The ashes fell down on us night and day," Brian said, continuing. "We thought we'd be buried in the stuff. But that was nothing compared to the hunger. We were an isolated city. There was no food, no trade. People were starving to death by the tens of thousands. Disease wiped out even more of us."

Dani stopped pedaling. "Only six hundred of you

survived?" she asked, taking in the enormity of the loss.

Brian shook his head. "It was bad. But not that bad. There were still plenty of us alive, but the little bit of farming we could do outside the city couldn't feed all the survivors. It made sense for most everyone to migrate into the southern Rockies, where the firestorms hadn't hit. It was still mostly green there. There were animals to be raised, gardens to be grown, fresh water to be had. Back in Denver it's bone dry. The storms always dump their loads in the mountains. We send crews out once a week to bring back fresh snow; that's our water supply."

"Why did you and the others stay?" questioned Dani.

"The city is still important. Those of us who stayed felt that there ought to be a central place where people could come to trade, find a doctor, have their disputes settled. Denver isn't what it used to be," he said. "Or actually, maybe it's *exactly* what it used to be back in the Old West. We're the fort in the wilderness where people come when they feel threatened. We've even got a warning bell in a church steeple like they had in the old days. You might say we're an outpost of civilization. For all we know, there may not be another place like this left in America."

It was getting dark, but Dani was enjoying their talk and didn't want to stop. She started pedaling again, saying, "You're pretty smart. Did you go to college?"

"Two years before the war."

"I bet you did real well in school."

"Not bad. Not that it means anything now," he added.

Matt felt the steady rhythm of Herbie's gait on the hard surface of the highway. He opened his eyes and saw the road passing below him. *I guess I'm alive,* he thought to himself. *But what am I doing upside down?* He turned his head and saw a bicycle rolling down the highway. And then he heard the voices.

"I didn't tell you before, but I was going to be an actress," Dani admitted with a nervous laugh.

"You're pretty enough," came the simple response from a male voice.

Matt blinked. *Who's that?* Confused, Matt watched Dani as she turned to look at a man riding a bike beside her. She didn't say anything. She just looked at the guy.

Except he was looking right past her. "What is it?" she asked him.

"Over there," he answered tightly, pointing to the darkening southeast. "On the horizon. Maybe ten miles away. See the moving lights?"

Matt was facing the wrong way and couldn't see a thing.

"I'm not sure," Dani said.

Brian took a pair of binoculars out of his backpack, peered through them, and then handed them to Dani. "Take another look," he said grimly.

It was a gang of men on motorcycles. The real slave traders. And they were moving fast, heading straight toward Brian, Dani, and Matt.

Chapter 13 ⸺

BRIAN GRIPPED THE HANDLEBARS OF HIS TEN-SPEED AND declared, "We've got to make a run for it."

"It's impossible," Dani replied. "Matt's too sick."

"He'll have to hold out the best he can. It'll be hard for him, but these freaks won't have any use for anyone who's sick; they'd murder Matt for the clothes on his back. As for us, they'll trade us for a few gallons of gasoline. So let's move it."

Matt cleared his throat, and in a hoarse whisper that surprised him, he said, "I like these clothes on my back, so go as fast as you can."

Dani and Brian whipped their heads around at the sound of Matt's voice.

"You're awake!" Dani cried, cycling back toward him and Herbie.

"If you can call it that," he said. "But blood's rushing to my head. Could you untie me?"

Brian and Dani cut the ropes, and woozy and weak, Matt sat up on Herbie's back. He said to Brian, "I don't know who you are, but it looks like you're on our side. If you say those guys back there aren't, let's get as far away from them as we can."

"Sounds good to me," said Brian.

"You sure you can make it?" Dani asked, deeply worried that Matt would tumble out of the saddle just as he had a few days earlier.

Matt had his doubts. He felt as if he weighed a total of twenty pounds, with all of it concentrated in his forehead. It was an effort for him just to hold the reins. But he didn't want to think about how he'd feel if that gang caught up to them. "I'll manage," he said. "Don't worry. Just get going."

Brian set the pace, and it was a fast one. Dani had trouble keeping up. And so did Herbie. As the horse galloped after the bicycles, Matt could do nothing but hang on.

The harsh bouncing up and down in the saddle brought Matt's nausea back. He retched and turned his head, throwing up water. His foot slipped out of the stirrup, but he didn't fall.

He leaned forward over the neck of his horse, trying to steady himself. "Don't make any surprise turns, Herb," he gasped.

The horse pricked up his ears.

Matt patted Herbie's neck and then grabbed the animal's mane. "If you don't mind, Herb," he added breathlessly, feeling his stomach heaving, "I'll hold on to this for a while."

The familiar touch and smell of the horse's hair had a calming effect on Matt's queasy stomach. He stayed in the saddle and didn't throw up anymore.

A short while later dusk gave way to night, and darkness descended. Brian, Matt, and Dani couldn't see and had to stop. The bikers had gotten much closer, but they still seemed to be several miles away. With their headlights on, however, it wouldn't take them long to catch up.

Suddenly, though, the distant sound of their droning engines died, and their headlights blinked off.

"What's going on?" Dani asked. "Why did they stop?"

"They know they've got us," Brian replied grimly. "They don't have to risk driving their bikes at night. Besides, these guys are animals; they like to toy with their victims. This is just their way of making us squirm."

"Well, they're sure doing a good job of it," Dani said.

Dani and Brian got off their bicycles and then helped Matt get down out of the saddle.

"I could use some water," Matt said.

"You can use more than that," said Brian, handing Matt a salt tablet. "Take this with your drink. It'll help."

Matt gratefully took the pill and swallowed it. "Listen," he said with a weak smile. "The suspense is killing me—"

"You mean the motorcycle gang back there?" interrupted Brian.

"No, you. Who are you?"

Brian laughed. "Just a dumb guy who got talked into leaving my safe home."

Dani immediately jumped to Brian's side and announced, "How's that for modesty? Brian, here, risked his life to save you, and he won't even take credit for it."

Matt looked at the way Dani was admiring Brian, and the way Brian was enjoying that admiration. He had a queasy feeling again in his belly, but it wasn't from the food poisoning. Just the same, he stuck out his right hand and offered it to Brian.

They shook hands. It took about all of Matt's strength, but he made sure that his grip was as strong as Brian's.

"Now that the introductions are out of the way," said Dani, "we'd better figure out what we're going to do. I don't know about you guys, but I'm not looking forward to the morning."

"First thing we'll do is give Matt another shot of his medicine," said Brian. "After that, we can rest for a while and then try to follow the highway in the dark. We won't get far, but at least we'll put a few more miles between us and the goons back there."

They all instinctively looked back in the direction of their pursuers. They were surprised to see the flicker of a fire in the distance. The bikers were obviously making themselves dinner.

"You know," said Matt thoughtfully, "if they had had those bikes on full throttle, they could have caught us before dark."

"Why should they waste their precious gas?" countered Brian bitterly. "It's hard enough to come by. The point is, their fuel will last twice as long at a

84

slower speed, and they know we can't outrun them. It's another half day to Denver."

"Denver," whispered Matt, rolling the name on his tongue as if he could taste it. "Then there really is a city left standing?"

"I saw it with my own eyes," Dani said excitedly. "Brian was telling me that only six hundred people are left, but the place is still in one piece. Tall buildings, courthouses, hospitals, everything still exists. You'll go nuts when you see it. It's like—well—*nostalgic.*"

Brian laughed. "Looks like you're rather fond of our city."

"Yeah," she admitted. "I guess I am." Then she slumped to the ground and muttered, "I just hope I'll get to see it again."

"You will," promised Matt with a sudden smile. "I've got an idea."

Chapter 14

Those guys back there," said Matt, gesturing toward the distant campfire, "can't catch us without their motorcycles."

"That's obvious," Brian said crisply. "What's your point?"

For some reason Matt enjoyed being one step ahead of Brian. He smiled, but still breathing heavily, said, "The point is, they think we're running away from them. The last thing they'd ever expect is for us to sneak up on them at night and slash their bike tires."

"You better lie down, Matt," said Brian sarcastically. "I think you're still delirious."

"Wait a minute," Dani said, cutting in. "That's not a bad idea. We could work our way to them in the dark by heading toward their campfire. It just might work."

"Are you crazy, also?" Brian asked, exasperated. "If they caught us near their bikes, we'd be dead meat in six seconds."

"We're going to be dead meat in the morning, anyway," Matt wheezed. "At least this way we'll have a chance."

Brian was silent, thinking. He hated to admit it, but Matt had a good point. That didn't mean, though, that Brian couldn't turn this situation to his advantage—at least as far as Dani was concerned.

"All right," said Brian graciously. "It's a good idea."

Matt looked up, startled by Brian's sudden turn-around. Although Brian was only a few feet away, Matt couldn't see him because of the darkness. It was too bad; he wanted to read the expression on his face.

"You two wait here," Brian said. "I'll go back along the interstate and see what I can do about those motorcycles."

So, that's the punch line, Matt realized. *The guy wants to be a hero. Well, I'll just see about that.*

"Forget it, Brian," Matt said sharply. "You're a city boy. Dani and I have a lot more experience at moving around in the dark. We'll take care of this. You just stay here and look after Herbie."

"Don't be ridiculous," Dani declared. "You're in no condition, Matt, to hike all those miles back and forth in the dark. You need to rest. Brian and I will do the dirty work. You stay here, look after Herbie, and light a fire so Brian and I can find our way back."

"Hey, you're not leaving me behind," Matt persisted.

"Forget it. No way," Dani shot back. "You're so

88

worn out you can barely breathe and talk at the same time. Brian and I will go. End of discussion."

"Really," Brian offered gallantly, "I can do this alone. I wouldn't want you to be in any danger, Dani."

If Matt had wanted to see Brian's face before, he would have killed to see Dani's. What was she thinking? Why didn't she say anything? The silence was charged with a meaning that scared Matt more than the motorcycle gang.

Finally, after what seemed like an hour but had only been three seconds, Dani softly said, "That's— very nice of you, Brian. But I can't let you fight our battles for us. You've done so much for us already. I'm going with you."

Brian grinned in the darkness.

They had been gone a long time, or so it seemed to Matt. After they left, he gathered kindling from the side of the road and piled it up so that later he could set the signal fire. Despite his best efforts, he dozed off from time to time, the sickness still within him. Following Brian's instructions, he eventually took another salt tablet and drank more water. It was a good sign that he was beginning to feel hungry for solid food.

It was a bad sign, however, that Dani seemed to like Brian.

Matt realized that Brian had saved his life, but that didn't stop him from feeling jealous. If anything, it made it worse for Matt, because he couldn't out-and-out dislike the guy. In the end, though, it didn't matter how he felt about Brian. What mattered was what Dani felt about him.

"I count eight," Dani whispered.

"Yeah. And it looks like most of them are asleep," added Brian.

They were lying flat on their bellies on a small rise about twenty yards from the gang's camp. The motorcycles were standing in a haphazard line at the edge of the firelight. It was going to be hard to get near the bikes without being noticed.

"How about a distraction?" Brian suggested. "I'll throw a rock over to the other side of the camp. When they all go to check it out, we can slash the tires."

"Bad idea," said Dani. "Now, there are only two of them awake. We do that, and all eight of them will be up. Too dangerous."

"Makes sense," he replied, impressed with her clearheaded thinking. If she was scared, it sure didn't show.

"I guess we just wait and hope the other two nod off, huh?" he said.

"You got it."

The only way of knowing that a long time had passed was that the gang's campfire had nearly gone out. It was only then that the last of the men had climbed into his blankets and gone to sleep.

Brian and Dani waited until the fire had turned to

embers before they began to crawl forward. They moved a few inches at a time. The sound of their hands and knees scraping along the ground seemed thunderously loud to their own ears, but the gang members obviously didn't hear it.

Brian and Dani were sweating from the tension when they reached the first bike. Brian held it steady while she slit through the heavy rubber with her blade.

They heard a barely audible *hisssss* as the bike settled down at a new angle. There was no point in cutting both the front and rear tires of each bike. One tire per motorcycle would do the trick. They wanted to do their dirty work and get out of there as fast as possible.

They slashed the tires of five more bikes. Two more to go.

But suddenly one of the gang members, a scrawny man in a filthy sweatshirt, sat up in his blankets. He shivered and threw more kindling onto the fire, the embers flaring up into bright flame.

The flame illuminated Brian and Dani.

"Intruders in the camp!" screamed the gang member.

The seven other men jumped out of their blankets and reached for their chains, knives, and guns.

Dani was sure it was all over for them. But there was no way she wasn't going to do her worst before they got their hands on her. She slashed the tire of the motorcycle in front of her and then rushed to the last bike to finish her work.

"No!" shouted Brian.

Dani lifted her head and saw Brian sitting on the bike. He flicked the headlight on, then jumped down on the kick start. The motorcycle came alive with a roar. He grabbed Dani and she swung onto the seat behind him.

A pistol shot tore at Brian's shirt. He ignored it. They zoomed out of the camp as yet another shot went wildly over their heads.

They disappeared into the darkness.

Matt couldn't see the motorcycle gang's fire anymore. It had faded into the black night. So much time had passed, it had to be nearly dawn.

Where are they? Matt kept asking himself. Despite how rotten he felt, Matt started to pace. *If that guy lets anything happen to Dani, I'll beat the crap out of him,* Matt vowed. He didn't care that Brian was taller and broader than he was. All he cared about was Dani.

The echo of a gunshot brought him up short. It was quickly followed by yet another faint boom. Seconds passed. Matt realized he had stopped breathing.

It looked bad. Real bad. But Matt couldn't do anything except follow the plan. He lit the campfire, hoping that Dani and Brian were still alive.

Suddenly he spotted a light moving in the blackness. And soon, he heard the faint sound of a motorcycle's engine above the crackle of the campfire. His heart sank. All he had done was to lead Dani's killers to him. *Well,* he thought, *they're going to pay a heavy price for what they've done.*

He pulled his knife from its scabbard on his belt and stood his ground.

Ten minutes later Brian and Dani skidded to a stop in front of Matt's fire riding a huge Harley-Davidson. Dani had her arms around Brian's waist, holding on to him with a huge smile plastered on her face.

Chapter 15

THEY TIED THE TWO BICYCLES TO THE HANDLEBARS OF the Harley-Davidson. Brian climbed back on the motorcycle to drive, and Dani told Matt to get on behind Brian.

He refused—it was a matter of pride. Instead, despite his illness and Dani's pleading, he rode Herbie all the way to downtown Denver.

Brian had a tumultuous greeting from his mother and friends. He had shown that his belief in Dani was justified, he had saved Matt's life, and he had ridden home on a motorcycle stolen from the slave traders. The doctor's son had been popular before, but now he was a certified hometown hero.

From his vantage point in the local hospital, however, Matt didn't see anything after the initial welcome home. Dr. Stoddard immediately tucked him into bed and gave him medicine, plenty of liquids, and three hot meals a day.

But by his third day in Denver, Matt became aware of something peculiar. The doctor was watching him too closely. She sat on a chair next to his bed, looking at his medical chart.

"If you really want to know how I'm feeling," Matt finally said, "why don't you just ask me? I'm not unconscious."

The plump, middle-aged woman smiled, enjoying Matt's direct, no-nonsense manner. "All right," she replied, putting down the chart. "So, how are you?"

"Curious."

"About what?"

"About how much time you spend here with me," he said. "I hear people talking about you—you're a big deal. Why are you hanging out with me so much? I don't care what those papers say," he added, pointing at the medical chart. "I may be weak, but I'm not that sick."

She inched her chair nearer to the bed and looked at Matt, studying his face.

"Want to know the truth?" she said.

Matt suddenly wondered if maybe he was more ill than he realized, but he refused to show any fear. He nodded for her to go on, holding his breath as he steeled himself for her news.

"I want to understand you," she said simply. "You and Dani are the talk of Denver. You're survivors and fighters. I'm curious like everyone else."

Matt quietly let out a sigh of relief. He wasn't going to die after all.

"Have I embarrassed you?" she asked when Matt didn't offer a comment.

"No," he said, gathering his wits. "It's just sort of a

funny thing for you to say. I mean, aren't *you* a survivor? Didn't all of you have to fight and scrap to stay alive, too?"

"Sure," Dr. Stoddard said, frowning. "But none of us has done what you and Dani did. You've traveled two thousand miles across a devastated land. Why didn't you stop at the first decent place that offered food and shelter?"

"We're trying to get to California, and—"

"Dani explained that before," said the doctor impatiently, cutting him off. "But why did you keep going after you saw what you were up against?"

"I can only speak for myself," he said. "I never thought of stopping—not seriously. I have to keep going."

The woman gently placed her hand on his shoulder. She was about to ask him another question when he surprised her by throwing a question at her instead. "Why did you decide to stay here in Denver? I mean, so many people migrated to the south. What made you choose to stay here?"

She had never thought of her young patient as an equal—yet he clearly felt that he was, and he spoke to her that way. *Perhaps,* it occurred to her, *what makes him a survivor is that he sees himself as an equal to every person that comes his way.*

"Have I embarrassed you?" he asked with just the hint of a smile.

"No," she said, quickly recovering. "I was just thinking. I guess the answer to your question is that I stayed here in Denver because I buried my husband

and two of my children here." She stopped for a moment and became reflective. Her professional veneer fell away. "Most people," she said, "left because their loved ones died here. For me, it's been an anchor. I don't want to go. Home isn't where you hang your hat, it's where you bury your dead."

"I'm sorry," Matt said softly. "I didn't mean to bring up sad memories."

"That's okay. They aren't sad. It's good to remember Henry and the girls. I should think of them more often—that's how they stay alive for me."

Matt put his hand over the woman's as it rested on his shoulder. "I'm glad you've still got your son," he offered.

Dr. Stoddard fought back her tears. "I'm glad, too," she said.

Later, after she had left Matt, Dr. Stoddard wondered for a minute who was the patient and who was the doctor.

Dr. Stoddard spent more time with Matt than Dani did. Just the same, Dani did visit him every afternoon. He noticed that she had new clothes, her hair was combed and pulled back from her face, and she had a healthy glow from good food and plenty of rest. He might have enjoyed the new Dani, except that on every visit she told him tales of "Brian this" and "Brian that." He had nothing against the guy. In fact, he knew he owed Brian his life. But just the same, Matt had had it.

"I'll be out of here soon," he told her on the fifth day. "I'm feeling a lot better."

"That's great!"

"Yeah, well, make sure the horses are ready to travel, because when I'm up and around, we're out of here."

Dani hunched her shoulders as if she were warding off a cold wind. "We'll talk about it later," she said.

"What's there to talk about?" asked Matt. "California is just over those mountains. With a little luck, we'll be there by the end of the summer. We'll leave in a couple of days."

In a timid voice she said, "I hate to say this—" She stopped, unable to go on.

"You hate to say what?" he prodded. "Since when can't you talk to me?"

"It's just that—well, tens of thousands of people have migrated into the mountains, Matt. Lots of these people come back to Denver and report what they've seen or heard."

"So?" Matt asked, waiting for her to get to the point.

"Nobody," she reluctantly continued, "has ever been to California and come back alive."

Matt looked at her blankly for a moment. Then the full meaning of what she had said finally hit him. If it were true, then his mother, father, and brother were certainly dead.

His mind reeled at the thought, not wanting to believe it.

"What about the rumors that California hadn't been hit?" he demanded.

"I guess that's all they were. Just rumors," Dani said gently.

"But we've come so far," he said in a whisper. "Are you sure?"

"That's what Brian says," she announced.

"Brian!" He suddenly exploded. "What does he know about California? How come he has all the answers? His mother never said anything about California to me. What makes him such an authority?" Matt's eyes burned with an intensity Dani had never seen before. "Why do you believe everything *he* says?" Matt thundered on, out of control.

Dani didn't know what to say. She started to back out of the room.

A brand-new thought took shape in Matt's brain. He switched mental gears and started to laugh.

"Are you all right?" Dani asked worriedly, stepping back toward the side of his bed.

He took her hand. "Don't you understand?" he said happily. "Of course no one's come back from California. Think about it. Why would anyone risk crossing the Rockies to come back here if California turned out to be a great place to live? They'd be crazy to leave!"

"I—I suppose you're right," Dani said with less enthusiasm than Matt expected.

"Of course I'm right," he declared. "And you'll see the proof of it yourself when we get there."

"I don't know," said Dani with a deep sigh. "I don't

100

know that I want to risk it. Those mountains look like trouble, and I'm tired of trouble. And the truth is," she blurted out, "I like it here! This is a real community. There are all kinds of things to do, and people to talk to. And Matt, they even put on plays to fill the time whenever there's a bad stretch of weather."

Yeah, and Brian Stoddard is here, Matt thought to himself bitterly.

"Give Denver a chance," implored Dani. "That's all I ask. You haven't really seen it yet. Just don't make your mind up about leaving yet, okay?"

Matt hemmed and hawed, but finally agreed. "A week," he said. "I'll give it a week."

"Everyone works in Denver," said Brian. "We all have jobs. And your job, Matt, will be to join a repair crew. A lot of important buildings are crumbling. It's dangerous work," Brian added. "Earthquakes have damaged a lot of the buildings and some of them are pretty unstable."

"The earthquake damage is no surprise," Matt replied. "There've been earthquakes all over the country."

"So I've learned from Dani," Brian said with a smile as he gave her an admiring glance. "I've been writing down everything she's seen since the night of the war."

"I know," Matt said in a low voice.

"I'd do the same with you," Brian continued, "but it'd probably be a waste of time since you both saw pretty much the same things."

"That's right," agreed Matt, smiling at Dani. "We've been together since the very beginning."

Brian frowned. Somehow he had to separate Matt and Dani. He wanted Dani for himself. But as it was, every other sentence Dani spoke was, "When Matt and I did this" and "When Matt and I did that."

It was too bad that Matt and Brian didn't compare notes.

____ Chapter 16 ____

WHO'S THE NEW GUY?" ASKED A BURLY FIFTEEN-year-old kid with straight, stringy black hair.

"Somebody said he's the guy Brian brought back, but I doubt it," came the reply from a tall twenty-year-old in a Bronco's sweatshirt. "He doesn't look like much."

The head of the six-person work group, a muscular thirty-two-year-old named Kogan—with the nickname Kogan the Barbarian—didn't say anything to Matt except, "Do your work, keep your mouth shut, and I won't have any trouble with you."

Matt felt anything but at home. He was an outsider and he knew it. It would take a long time before he was accepted by these people. And he wasn't sure he even wanted their acceptance.

Their job that day was to repair a wooden walkway high in a church steeple so another crew could stand on it the next day to patch the holes in the steeple roof.

"Be careful," Kogan warned his crew as they as-

103

cended the stairs. "If any of you accidentally rings this bell," he said, pointing to it, "I guarantee that the next thing that gets rung will be your neck!"

Matt waited for Kogan to continue climbing before he tapped the shoulder of the kid with the black, stringy hair, who was just ahead of him.

"You want something?"

"Yeah. What happens when the bell's rung?"

The kid with the black hair laughed. "The place goes crazy," he said. "It's our warning bell and when it sounds, everybody drops everything and runs straight for Mile High Stadium. That's where we meet in an emergency."

"Has the bell ever been rung?" Matt asked, continuing his climb.

"Sure. Four times so far, but two of them turned out to be false alarms. And let me tell you, those false alarms really bent everyone out of shape. When you hear that bell, it's supposed to mean big trouble. There are six hundred and twelve people in Denver, and we all shake when we hear it ring."

"Thanks for the info," said Matt with a nod.

"Sure. No problem." The kid cleared his throat and gave Matt a questioning look. "Are you the guy that Brian Stoddard brought back?"

"Yeah," Matt said guardedly. "What of it?"

"Tell me the truth, did you really come from New Jersey?"

"It's the truth," said Matt.

"Really?"

"Really."

"Wow, I bet you've got some stories to tell. By the way"—he stuck out his right hand—"my name is Vic Minetti."

Matt shook Minetti's hand. It was a start.

"We've got to make this more secure," Kogan the Barbarian announced when they reached the rotting wooden platform above the bell at the top of the tower. "Another repair crew is coming in tomorrow, so we've got to finish our work today. Understand?"

Several members of the crew grunted, and that seemed good enough for Kogan. Meanwhile, two of the workers began stacking the lumber they'd been carrying up the stairs.

Standing at the edge of the walkway, Matt glanced down and saw the large flat-top of the iron bell. It didn't hang from a center ring, but rather from a metal superstructure. Four steel rods were securely fastened to the four walls of the belfry, creating a sort of cradle for the bell.

The repair team worked all morning with hammers and saws, stripping the old wood away and replacing it with sturdier lumber they had salvaged from other buildings. Unlike the rest of the crew, though, Matt had to take frequent breaks. He was still weak from his illness and couldn't keep up the pace.

When it came time for their lunch break, Kogan dismissed everyone—except Matt. "You're staying here," he ordered. "Keep working. Nobody eats who doesn't do their share."

"Give him a break," Minetti called out. "It's his first day."

"Stuff it, Minetti," thundered Kogan. "I run this crew, and we've got a job to do. I won't stand for slackers. If he can't do the work, he shouldn't be here."

Matt smiled at Vic Minetti to thank him for the support. Then he nodded at Kogan and said, "You won't get any argument from me."

"Yeah, well, you'll get plenty of argument from me, though," Kogan shot back. "I'm staying up here with you to make sure you get your work done right. In other words, I don't get any lunch, either."

The others dropped their tools and left the platform to go downstairs. Matt kept on working as Kogan looked on with a disapproving glare.

Matt used the claw end of his hammer to lift up a small, rotting piece of wood. Then he extracted another small piece, trying to make room for one long strip of new lumber.

"At the rate you're going," Kogan said, disgusted, "we'll be here all day and all night. You've got to pull out bigger pieces." He knelt down next to Matt and, with his bare hands, tore at a big slab of wood at the edge of the platform, ripping it up. Kogan gave Matt a smile of triumph. "See?" he said. "That's how you get the job done!"

Now Matt knew how his crew boss got the nickname Kogan the Barbarian.

When Kogan turned to dump the unwieldy piece of

lumber, he accidentally swung the end around, right at Matt.

"Hey! Look out!" Matt yelled. But it was too late. It struck him in the face. He flew backward, and suddenly there was nothing beneath his feet. He had fallen off the platform!

He would have plunged to the bottom of the tower if the bell, itself, hadn't been in the way. Matt landed on his back, spread-eagled, right on top of it with a heavy thud. He landed so squarely in the center that the bell not only didn't ring, it didn't even move.

Kogan tried to help when he saw Matt start to fall. "Oh, my God!" he cried, dropping the piece of lumber in his hands and lunging forward to grab at Matt's clothing. But all that Kogan managed to do was lose his balance. As he fell face forward onto the platform, he dragged his right wrist across an up-turned nail. Blood gushed from the artery he had opened, spewing out like a red fountain. Kogan passed out at the sight of it.

He was bleeding to death, and there was no one there to help him.

Chapter 17

KOGAN, YOU JERK, THROW ME A ROPE!" MATT CALLED out.

There was no answer.

"Kogan!"

Something splashed on Matt's cheek. He touched the spot with his finger and looked at it. Blood.

"Kogan?" Matt called out again.

A steady stream of blood began to drip through the broken floorboards of the landing. Matt didn't know what had happened to Kogan, but he knew it wasn't good.

In other circumstances he would have stayed where he was and waited for the others to come back from their lunch break. He couldn't do that now. Not with Kogan bleeding like a river up there all alone.

Matt studied the metal structure that held the heavy iron bell in place. One of the four rods that connected the bell to a wall of the steeple led directly over the stairway, about fifteen feet away. The only way to get off the bell was to climb, hand over hand, along the rod and drop down onto the stairs.

As he grabbed hold of the metal beam with both hands and let himself dangle into space, he thought, *I hope Denver has a psychiatrist, because I need to have my head examined for doing this.*

Inching his way along the steel rod, he hoped to reach the relative safety of the far wall where he could jump down onto the stairs.

His arms were aching from the strain, and his hands instantly blistered from holding on to the rusty metal. Once committed, though, he had no choice but to go all the way—or fall to his death.

He had ten more feet to go.

He felt the fatigue in his muscles. He wasn't nearly so strong as he had been before he got sick.

Seven feet.

His fingers felt numb. He wasn't sure he could hold on much longer. But he had to keep moving.

Four feet.

He looked down, saw the huge drop, and got dizzy. *Don't do that!* he told himself. He tried to think of his best friend, Cliff, back in Fair Oaks. They used to climb the monkey bars in his backyard. *It was just like this. One hand over the other. Just make believe it's the same,* he kept telling himself.

Two feet.

His arms were giving out. It was now or never.

The stairs were just below and slightly to his right. Matt swung his body forward, let go of the steel rod, and closed his eyes. A mere second later, he slammed into the wall of the steeple and crumpled onto the stairs.

He rolled down at least six steps before he stopped —but he was alive. There was no time for self-congratulations, though. Matt immediately scrambled to his feet and rushed up the stairs to the landing.

It was then that he finally saw how close to death Kogan really was. The man had lost an enormous amount of blood. Matt jumped into action. He took off his belt and wrapped it tightly around Kogan's arm, high near the armpit. It shut off the flow of blood to the rest of the limb. The tourniquet seemed to help.

If he hasn't lost too much blood, Kogan just might make it, Matt thought. But right after the bleeding was under control, Kogan went into deep shock. The man simply stopped breathing.

"Oh, great," Matt groaned. He turned Kogan over and started giving him mouth-to-mouth resuscitation. *There must be at least three hundred women in Denver,* he complained to himself between breaths, *and I have to do this with the ugliest man in the entire city. Just my luck.*

It took almost two minutes, but Kogan's lungs finally sputtered back to work on their own. A short while after that, Matt heard the voices of the repair crew coming back up the stairwell.

"Get Dr. Stoddard!" Matt yelled down to them. "Hurry!"

Three members of the crew ran for help, while one of them hurried up the stairs to find out what was wrong.

The guy in the Denver Bronco's T-shirt was the one who first saw Kogan's bloody body lying on the walkway. He stared at Kogan and then at Matt. "If he dies, creep," vowed the guy in the T-shirt, "I'm going to kill you."

Matt just stared back at him, in almost as much shock as Kogan had been in.

Matt stood in the background while Dr. Stoddard finally brought Kogan back to consciousness. In front of everyone, the crew boss pleaded for understanding. "It was an accident," he said. "I didn't mean to kill the new guy." He babbled on, explaining in fits and starts what had happened. They couldn't shut him up. Finally Dr. Stoddard motioned for Matt to come forward.

Kogan thought he was delirious; he couldn't believe his eyes.

"How did you survive?" he gasped.

Matt told him everything. He didn't try to make what he had done any more or less heroic than it was. He told it straight, then he turned and walked out, not even looking at the guy in the Denver Bronco's T-shirt.

He had been vindicated, but Matt resented that he had been accused in the first place. Angrily he stormed over to the high school gymnasium where he had been given a bed. He shared that sleeping space with fifty-nine other guys. Nobody was around, however, in the middle of the afternoon when Matt returned there to clean himself up and change his sweat- and blood-soaked clothes.

When he left the high school, he marched several blocks to the place where Brian was working that day, writing down Dani's recollections of her two-thousand-mile journey across America.

Matt didn't bother to knock. He slammed open the door and marched right in. He found Brian standing behind Dani, rubbing her neck and shoulders.

"I see you're both hard at work," Matt said sharply.

"As a matter of fact, we are," Dani shot back angrily. "We've been at it almost all day without a break. And speaking of work, what are you doing here?" she asked, embarrassed that her friend wasn't showing the proper appreciation for all that Brian and the people of Denver had done for the two of them. "How come you're not doing your job? We owe these people a lot."

"I figure my debt to Denver is repaid," Matt replied without explaining. "And I figure you've repaid both of our debts to Brian all by yourself."

Dani jumped to her feet. "What is that supposed to mean?" she demanded.

"Figure it out yourself," he said, and then he spun around, stomped out, and slammed the door behind him.

Matt was immediately sorry he had opened his big mouth. He wasn't angry at Dani, he was just afraid he was losing her. Perhaps he already had. But why couldn't she see that he needed to talk to her?

Matt did need to talk to someone. Although there were six hundred and twelve people in Denver, he still didn't have anybody he could share his feelings with. That's why he made his way to the stable. Herbie and Whisk whinnied their welcome.

Matt patted their heads. At least there was someone in this so-called civilization who was glad to see him.

Chapter 18

LATE THAT NIGHT, WHILE FIRES BURNED THROUGHOUT the city, Matt walked the streets, trying to decide what to do.

There was something awesomely beautiful yet painfully sad about the tall, empty buildings glowing in the firelight. Matt gazed at the structures and marveled at the towering monuments to the ability of man. Yet man had really flopped when it had counted.

And so had Matt.

He was sure that Dani would never leave with him now. He had acted like a jerk. When he had done stupid things in the past, he had always had a chance to make up for it. He had been, in a manner of speaking, the last guy on earth. Dani couldn't choose another boy instead of him because she didn't have any other choice. But not anymore.

Brian had come along. *Okay, the guy did save my life,* Matt thought to himself. *Fine. I appreciate that. I really do. But that doesn't mean I have to like the guy.*

And it doesn't mean I have to smile every time I see him with Dani.

The thought of seeing Dani and Brian together for the rest of his life made Matt wince. He couldn't possibly stand that kind of humiliation. Something had to give. And as he walked the streets, looking at the ghostly buildings, he knew what he had to do. Yes, something had to give. *He* had to give—give something to Dani: her freedom.

He stopped then and looked around at the greatness that had once been. Maybe the six hundred people who remained would bring new glory to this city. Maybe they could create a new society out of the ashes and the rubble. He hoped so. But they'd have to do it without him.

This is what Dani wants, he realized. *Everything that I can't give her, she can find right here. Safety, people to talk to, a home. She'll have a chance to be in plays here, something she had thought would never be possible. And she'll have Brian.*

That was what hurt the most.

But if Matt was lucky and managed to cross the Rockies all alone, and if the rumors about California were true and his family was still alive, then Matt wouldn't be alone anymore. Dani would have everything that she had always wanted, and he'd have everything that he had always wanted. Well—almost everything.

Matt walked slowly back to the high school gymnasium. The place was silent except for snoring and a few people crying quietly in their dreams. By torch-light, Matt found his cot. He pulled his backpack out from under the bed and rummaged through it, look-ing for a pencil and a piece of paper.

He found what he was looking for and wrote a farewell note.

Dear Dani,

I'm not much on writing; I just don't have the nerve to say this to you in person. But my mind is made up. Denver is a good place for you—I can see that. The problem is, it's no good for me. I know I promised that I'd give it a week, but I just can't do it. I don't fit in here. So, I'm taking Herbie and heading to California to find my family.

You want to know the truth? I'm going to miss you. I'll think about you every day. The fact is, I'll probably never stop thinking about you. I guess, in my own stupid way, I love you. There, I said it. And it's the truth.

I'm sorry about busting in on you and Brian the way I did. It was dumb. Be happy, Dani. And please, try not to forget me.

Matt

He walked to the stable and left the note under-neath Whisk's brush, knowing that Dani came by there every morning to look after her horse. She'd find the message long after he had gone.

He saddled up Herbie, took his possessions, one day's worth of food, a canteen full of water, and rode out of Denver at first light.

Telling himself not to look back, Matt rode toward the Rockies. But in the foothills west of Denver, Matt couldn't help himself. He turned in his saddle and stared at the city glittering in the light of a new day. Dani was there. And he'd never see her again.

He rubbed the moisture away from his eyes, telling himself that the tears had been caused by the light from the rising sun.

"Let's go, Herbie," he said in a choked voice. "It's just you and me now."

"I understand why you like Dani," Brian's mother said to her son as they walked toward the hospital. "And I heartily approve. She's a breath of fresh air. It's just that I think you ought to be careful with your heart," she advised. "She may not be that easy to win."

"I'll get her," Brian said confidently.

"I hope you do. Just don't forget that you're not the only boy in her life."

"Hey, Matt's no problem," he said. "The guy really blundered yesterday, and Dani is mad as hell at him. I'm doing better with her every day. In a couple of weeks Matt will be just an old boyfriend. You'll see."

His mother smiled. "You're kind of cocky, aren't you?"

"You raised me to be a winner, Mom."

Dr. Stoddard shook her head. "A winner isn't

somebody who always wins; a winner is also a person who knows when he can't win."

"I'll leave the losing for the next guy—like Matt."

"You know I'm rooting for you, Brian, but don't sell Matt short. He's got a lot of character."

"I know," he admitted. "Dani talks about him all the time. But what else is she going to talk about? He's practically the only person she's known since the war. But Denver has really opened her eyes. She has possibilities here she never had before—and one of those possibilities is me."

They were almost at the hospital when Brian saw Dani heading down a side street toward the stable. Dr. Stoddard saw her, too. "You know," she said wistfully, "it's too bad you and Matt are both after Dani. If she didn't stand between the two of you, I bet you and he could be great friends."

"Maybe," agreed Brian. "It's too bad we'll never know. Got to go now, Mom. See you later."

"Say hello to Dani for me," she called out, seeing the direction in which her son was heading.

Chapter 19

BRIAN OPENED THE STABLE DOORS, SAYING, "I WAS JUST talking to my mother and I saw you heading— Hey! What are you doing?"

With tears running down her face, Dani had just finished saddling Whisk. "I'm going after Matt," she wailed. "He's left for California without me."

Brian ran up to Dani and pulled her away from her horse. "You can't go after him," he insisted. "You'd never find him. He could be anywhere. You'll die out there alone."

"I've got to go after him," she whimpered.

"I won't allow it," he said imperiously. "If Matt didn't want to stay, that was his business. But this is your home now, Dani. You belong here."

"I belong with Matt," she cried, breaking free of Brian. She ran to Whisk and started climbing up into the saddle. Brian pulled at her legs, shouting, "This is crazy! Stay here with me!"

The tug on her legs made Dani lose her balance. Her toe came out of the stirrup, and she fell backward, banging her head against the side of Whisk's stall.

Matt rode slowly at first, half hoping that Dani would come riding out after him. But Dani never showed up.

Slumped in the saddle, Matt picked up his pace and rode up into the Rockies. The mountain range had once been a symbol of hope to him, but now that he had finally reached this milestone in his journey, he felt empty.

The barren, scorched mountains in front of him matched his mood. A few weeds were sprouting through the burnt earth, but the ground was more black and rusty brown than it was green. It was like that all the way to the north. Matt knew that he'd have to head due south if he was going to try to live off the land.

He took Herbie down a rise, toward a narrow path that ran parallel to both the city and the looming mountain range. Matt figured he'd follow it south until the Rockies turned green again. But at the bottom of the rise, instead of the *clip-clop* of hooves on hard ground, he heard a soft, squishy sound. He looked down and saw that Herbie's hooves were covered with mud.

Matt looked up at the towering mountains above him. They were laden with millions of tons of snow and ice. It had been so cold ever since the war that nothing at the higher elevations could melt. At least, that's what he had heard back in Denver. Finding this wet ground so close to the city was very strange. If all that snow up in the mountains started melting . . .

Matt shivered at the thought.

There wasn't any way he could leave if Dani was in danger. But was she? He had to find out.

Matt turned around and followed the path north as it wound higher and farther up through the foothills into the lower reaches of the Rockies. Denver sat off to his right, looking small and vulnerable down below.

At first the ground was merely wet. Later, the path was cut by a little stream flowing down out of the mountains. Riding uphill, traveling on slick, muddy ground, made for a difficult, slow ride. The morning had long since passed, and it was late in the afternoon now.

Matt left the path and urged Herbie to climb in the direction from which the stream was coming. Soon, the stream widened and deepened.

"That's a lot of water considering nothing is supposed to be melting," Matt mumbled to himself. He remembered how the temperature seemed to be rising during the last couple of weeks. And then he remembered how fast the hailstones had melted back at the truck stop. The air was definitely warming up.

Matt stared at the muddy water heading swiftly down the mountainside. There wasn't a tree or a bush or even a patch of grass to stop or absorb its flow. So the water took the muddy earth along for the ride, heading where gravity took it: to the high plains below—to Denver.

They'll be glad to get the water, Matt thought to himself. *Unless they get more than they bargained for.*

Matt was getting worried. But it was too late to continue his journey. Riding was treacherous, even in the twilight, so he found some dry ground and fell into a troubled sleep. He dreamt that he was sitting in a movie theater with Dani. He was sitting on her left. Just as he got up the courage to put his arm around her shoulder, he found that Brian—sitting on her right—had beaten him to it, and Dani was leaning her head against Brian's shoulder.

There were no monsters, no endless falls, but there was no doubt what it was—it was definitely a nightmare.

Matt woke up long before dawn, not feeling particularly rested. The dry ground he had chosen had turned wet and muddy during the night. As soon as there was enough light, he saddled Herbie and continued his climb.

He followed narrow trails, cutting back and forth, slowly heading higher and higher. He was several thousand feet above Denver, yet he could clearly see the city just to the south and east of him in the morning light.

Strangely, he wasn't all that cold. The temperature wasn't nearly so low as he had expected it to be at that elevation.

Herbie plodded through snowfields. The sunlight reflecting off the white surface was nearly blinding, but Matt noted that the snow underfoot was soft and wet. It was melting. From time to time he saw brown streams flowing down across the snow and ice.

Matt was growing more and more nervous. He was riding in a no-man's-land of stark devastation. Yet he continued on. Even if Dani ended up with Brian, he *had* to know that she was going to be safe. He owed her that much, at least.

The water and mud flowing downhill didn't seem to be getting any worse as Matt drew near the lip of a plateau. He started to think that maybe he had been worrying for nothing.

"Looks like Dani will get to take plenty of baths," he announced to Herbie. "I guess she'll like that. What's that you say? The water's a little dirty? No problem. Once the water gets to a lower elevation and collects in a pool, the dirt will settle to the bottom." Matt frowned, realizing that he'd be carrying on solo conversations such as that with Herbie for a long time to come. He was going to miss Dani—a lot.

Matt figured he'd climb to the crest of the plateau and take one quick look around. It was time he got out of there and on his way to the south. The bare mountainside, stripped of life by the firestorms, gave him the creeps. It was like being on a snow-covered moon.

"Just a little farther, Herbie," he said, taking yet another switchback in order to climb the last twenty yards to the top of the plateau.

Matt guided Herbie across the face of the slope, on

a slight incline, getting closer to the crest. But they were also curving around the mountain, seeing the plateau from an entirely different angle.

Matt heard it before he saw it. It was a roar, like a waterfall. Herbie balked at going any farther and wouldn't move despite the bootheels Matt jabbed in his flanks. "Be like that," Matt said angrily.

He dismounted and tied Herbie's reins around a small, snow-covered boulder. Matt continued around the curve, heading for the top just ten yards away. His feet sank into the soft snow and into the muddy ground below. But he kept on going.

And then he saw the source of the noise.

It wasn't a waterfall. It was more like a mudfall. Flowing down from the very crest of the plateau was a huge, steady cascade of heavy mud. It looked like a river of lava curling down from the top of a volcano, except it wasn't molten rock, it was ice-cold earth and water.

Matt finally glanced over the lip of the plateau to see where all that mud and water was coming from. The sight that filled his eyes literally took his breath away. And he knew that it could just as easily take his life away. And not just his own life. Dani was in terrible danger.

What he saw was a gigantic valley—he could barely see to the opposite side—that was completely filled with water. Ice and snow had obviously melted above it and had drained down into this massive lake. But a wall of the lake—just to the left of where he was standing—was beginning to break apart. It was as if a dam were about to collapse. When it did, millions of gallons of water and mud would flow down the mountain, burying everything and everyone in its path.

It didn't take a genius to know what path the wave of death would take. Since the day before, Matt had been following the very same path up the mountain. When the lake emptied, its contents would continue to flow in the same natural direction. In other words, Denver was destined to be buried by a tidal wave of muddy water!

Unless Matt could outrace it.

Chapter 20

SLIPPING AND SLIDING, MATT RAN BACK TO HERBIE. "I forgive you," he said, climbing up into the saddle. "You were right. This is no place for us, so let's get out of here."

It wasn't so easy. The slope was steep and the mud and snow made the footing difficult. Moving faster didn't help. Several times Herbie nearly lost his balance. It was frustrating. Matt wanted to race back to Denver, but he had to constantly cut back and forth across the slope to keep from tumbling down the mountainside.

He cursed himself for having taken such a leisurely trip on the way up. It was nearly noon and he had to reach Denver with enough time to sound the warning and get everyone to high ground.

Matt's immediate problem, though, was saving himself. If the side of the lake gave way soon, he'd be swept down to certain death. And from what he had seen, the edge of the lake was just about ready to break wide open.

He reached the snowfields where he had seen little brown streams. There were more of them now. And less and less snow. The land seemed slightly more level, so Matt let Herbie stretch out into a canter.

Big mistake.

Herbie suddenly slipped, sliding down the field on his haunches. Matt fell out of the saddle and rolled down the hill beside his horse in the snow and mud. Barely able to breathe, unable to see, Matt flailed with his hands and his feet, trying to find something to stop the fall. He and Herbie finally slammed into a snowdrift, abruptly ending their swift descent.

The horse shook himself off and staggered to his feet, blowing hard. Matt was soaking wet, muddy, and dazed. The net effect of the fall, however, was that they were much closer to a lower trail.

Matt tottered along as best he could on foot, leading Herbie to the path below, then he once again climbed up into the saddle. He thought the ride would be easier now. But he was wrong. The once-wet trail was now at least a foot thick with mud that had fallen from the crest of the overflowing lake above. It was like galloping through quicksand, but it was the only way back to Denver. To Dani.

Dani opened her eyes.

"How are you feeling?" Dr. Stoddard asked.

Dani held her head and groaned.

"It'll feel better in a little while. The ice will help. Just hold it against the bump."

"She'll be okay, won't she, Mom?" Brian asked anxiously.

"She might have a slight concussion, but it doesn't look like anything too serious. She'll be fine."

Dani was wondering what she was doing there, lying in the hospital with a headache. Suddenly it all came back to her. Despite the pain, she sat bolt upright and tried to climb out of her bed.

"Where do you think you're going?" Dr. Stoddard demanded.

"After Matt," she replied simply.

Stoddard and her son both pushed her back into the bed.

"You're not going anywhere," said the doctor. "Not with that bump. Besides," she said with sympathy, "Matt's long gone. You'd never catch up to him now."

"But I've got to."

"You can't," said Dr. Stoddard gently. "Might as well face up to it. I know the two of you have gone through a lot together, but that's over now. He's gone and the best thing—really, the only thing—you can do is to forget him and get on with your life here."

Brian was pleased with his mother's speech, but Dani wasn't. She burst into tears. The pain in her head was nothing compared to the pain in her heart.

Matt had been riding for hours, fighting the mud, the water, and his growing fear that at any moment a wall of brown slime was going to sweep down on him from behind and bury him. It was almost midafternoon, and he was near the bottom of the foothills.

Here, at last, the footing was better. Although his horse was tiring, Matt urged him on, and Herbie responded, stretching his long legs into a mile-eating gallop.

It wasn't long before the empty western suburban streets of Denver reverberated with pounding hooves. And soon the suburbs gave way to skyscrapers. Matt reached the perimeter of the inner city that was blocked by overturned cars, trucks, and buses. A Denver Defense Squad stood armed at the narrow entranceway.

There was no time for lengthy explanations. "Get out of the way!" he shouted.

There were five people, all of them armed, and they stood their ground.

Matt never slowed down. He barreled right past them, and they had to jump out of the way or get trampled. One of the guards shot an arrow at Matt; it flew harmlessly over his head. Another guard launched a spear that struck the ground right next to Herbie. A moment later Matt turned a corner and was out of sight.

Riding like a madman through the city streets of Denver, Matt was quite a sight. People turned to stare and others peered out of windows, watching this mud-covered horse and rider gallop past them.

Finally, he saw what he was looking for—the church steeple at the end of the street. "Almost there," Matt called out to Herbie. The horse's eyes bulged in their sockets, the animal straining for its master.

Just as they reached the front of the church, Matt pulled back on the reins and Herbie came to a grateful stop. Matt leaped off the horse's back, ran up the steps—three at a time—and charged into the darkened building.

He climbed three flights of stairs until he reached the bottom of the bell tower. The long, heavy rope hung down within his reach. . . .

Two Denver citizens, a man and a woman, were working nearby repairing a church wall. They hadn't noticed Matt, until they suddenly heard the loud clang of the bell. They spun around and the man yelled, "What the hell are you doing?"

Matt ignored him and kept ringing the bell, pulling on the rope as if his life depended on it. Which it did.

The man and the woman lunged at Matt, ripping his hands off the rope. They wrestled him to the ground and pinned him there.

"I'll hold him down," said the man, who easily weighed over two hundred pounds and had one of his knees on Matt's chest. "You go get the mayor."

"I will if I can find him," the woman replied. "This city is going to be pure bedlam."

"Just do the best you can." As the woman ran down the stairs, the man turned to Matt and said, "That was some stupid stunt you pulled. You're in real deep trouble, kid."

Chapter 21

DANI HADN'T MOVED IN SEVERAL HOURS, BUT BRIAN knew that she wasn't asleep. He could tell by her occasional sobs.

Like everyone else since the night of the war, Brian had had a hard life. He had no more tears left. He couldn't help it, but he resented Dani's ability to cry. After sitting in a chair next to her bed for half the afternoon, he was beginning to lose his patience. And finally he couldn't take it anymore. He stood up, leaned over her, and grabbed her shoulder, twisting her around to face him.

"I'm getting sick of all this sniveling," he said. "The guy isn't even dead. And from where I'm standing it seems to me you're a whole lot better off than he is. I'll take care of you. I've got power here. People respect me. You'll see, I'll protect you."

Dani's red-rimmed eyes opened wide. She pulled away from Brian and in a husky, angry voice said, "I don't need you as a protector. I can protect myself just fine, thank you. At least when I was with Matt, we protected each other. We were a team."

"You and I can be a team," he offered, leaning in close to her. "It's what I've always wanted. And unless I miss my guess," he said with confidence, knowing Matt was now out of her life, "I think you want it, too." And with that, he put his arms around her and kissed her.

She fought against him, trying to pull away. But Brian wouldn't let her go. Dani was no fluttery young woman, not after so many brutal months of trying to survive. But when she finally shoved Brian off, he fell over sideways, striking his head against the night table.

He slumped to the floor.

Just then the signal bell in the church steeple began to sound.

"Perfect," Dani said and sighed.

She jumped up, looked out a window, and saw people rushing out into the street, heading in the direction of Mile High Stadium.

Something terrible was happening.

Dani did everything she could think of to revive Brian, including throwing water in his face. Nothing worked. Then she got scared—maybe she'd killed him. No. He was still breathing and he had a steady heartbeat.

She ran into the street to get help. But by that time, everyone was gone; they were well on their way to the stadium. If she was going to find help for Brian, she'd have to go there, too.

136

Dani didn't see anybody as she ran down East Colfax Avenue. Eventually, she neared the bridge built over the dry riverbed that had once been the South Platte River. The South Platte was the dividing line between east and west Denver. Mile High Stadium was close to the other side of the riverbed. But before she crossed the bridge, a movement caught her eye. She turned and looked down a side street. There, in front of the church that housed the now silent signal bell, was Herbie!

Dani ran toward the horse.

Running down the same street from the opposite direction was a work group. They had obviously come a great distance and were rushing to get to the stadium.

"You're going the wrong way!" a man called out to Dani. He tried to grab her and turn her around.

"No!" she cried, dodging his clumsy attempt to snatch her arm. She ducked around Herbie and dashed into the church.

"She's gone crazy," muttered the man. "I'll get her and catch up to you," he told his co-workers.

"Let me up!" Matt shouted angrily at the guy who still had his knee on Matt's chest.

"Not till the mayor gets here. If this is a false alarm, the council is going to crucify you."

"This isn't a false alarm," insisted Matt. "I told you the truth. Look at me. Why would I roll around in the mud and come back here and tell you this story if it wasn't true?"

"What's going on here?" the mayor huffed as he arrived with a couple of other council members.

Before Matt could answer, Dani's voice, crying Matt's name, suddenly echoed inside the old church.

"Here! I'm up here!" Matt shouted, squirming under the weight of his jailer.

Dani bounded up the three sets of stairs to the landing, the workman still chasing after her. When she saw Matt, she ran to him, diving into his arms, mud and all.

"I never thought I'd see you again," she sobbed. "I'm so glad you came back."

"I had to come back," he said. "Denver is going to be buried under a mountain of water and mud. I—I was worried about you. It could happen anytime, Dani. There's a huge lake up in the mountains that's overflowing its banks. It's actually breaking down its banks. But this guy won't listen to me," he said, indicating his captor. "He thinks I'm lying."

The mayor looked concerned. He turned to a fellow councilman. "Maybe we should send out a team to check on it. What do you think?"

Matt shouted in frustration, "You're wasting valuable time! Please, you've got to trust me and get to high ground."

"This is highly irregular," said the mayor, unsure of what to do. "After all, we hardly know you."

The workman who had followed Dani had heard everything and was standing quietly in the shadows at the top of the landing. He cleared his throat and stepped forward. "Mr. Mayor?" he said.

Everyone turned and saw a young man in a Denver Bronco's T-shirt. "What are you doing here, Thomsen?" asked the city leader.

Matt and the man in the Bronco's T-shirt stared at each other. Then the fellow named Thomsen turned to face the mayor and said, "You need someone to vouch for Matt Chandler's character. And I'm your man. If he says Denver's in danger, I believe him."

The mayor and the other council members were surprised at Thomsen's declaration. Before they could question him any further, though, he had started running down the stairs.

"Where are you going?" demanded the mayor.

"Where do you think? I'm getting out of Denver and heading for the foothills. I can't swim worth a damn."

The mayor still seemed undecided.

"Look," said Matt. "I've given you the warning. Do what you want. Just let me get Dani out of here."

"Everyone's assembled at the stadium," suggested one of the council members. "Why don't we let the people decide for themselves?"

The mayor nodded. It seemed like the prudent thing to do.

They let Matt go, and he and Dani raced out of the church.

"Come on, let's get Whisk," said Matt. "There's no time to lose."

"No, wait," Dani announced. "We've got to get Brian. I knocked him out and he'll die in the flood if we don't get him out of here."

139

"Knocked him out?" Matt questioned.

"I'll tell you about it sometime. But not now."

Matt was silent for a moment.

"Well, are you going to help him, or not?" Dani demanded.

"I guess I owe him that, huh?"

Dani smiled.

"You get Whisk and I'll get Brian. Just tell me where he is."

Chapter 22

T HEY DRAPED BRIAN OVER HERBIE'S BACK AND TIED him down.

"Looks like he's leaving Denver almost the same way you arrived," Dani said.

"He hasn't left Denver yet," Matt said soberly. "And neither have we."

It was getting close to sundown, but they figured they'd have just enough light to reach the foothills. Herbie, at least, had had a little time to rest. Whisk was fresh, but he'd have to carry both Matt and Dani. It was going to be a struggle for both horses.

But they were finally on their way. Riding down East Colfax, they reached the bridge over the South Platte. There was a thin trickle of water in the riverbed that hadn't been there just an hour before.

Matt felt a chill. And then he felt something far worse. . . .

The ground began to tremble.

"It's happened," Matt said, the words sticking in

his throat. "The wall of the lake must've just given way."

They could see hundreds of people in the distance streaming toward the Rockies. Most, if not all, of the citizens of Denver had obviously decided to be safe rather than sorry. And they had felt the tremor, too. Matt and Dani could see them suddenly break into a panicked race toward the high ground.

No words were necessary now. Only speed.

Dani sat behind Matt in the saddle, but even with both of them on Whisk's back, they practically flew through the streets of Denver.

High up in the mountains, northwest of the city, a tidal wave of water and mud was cascading down toward them. They couldn't see it or hear it—*yet*—but it was coming. And when it came, it would be unforgiving.

By the time they reached the western suburbs of Denver, they had caught up to several dozen stragglers. Neither Matt nor Dani knew any of them, but this was no time for greetings. With faces etched with terror, men, women, and children raced to the foothills above the city. Some rode bicycles or horses. Others were in horse-drawn wagons. There were even two trucks loaded with the sick and injured that lumbered up into the foothills. No one was on foot—everyone was in a vehicle.

Matt and Dani raced along beside them, every step on the now wet and sloping ground growing harder for Herbie and Whisk. Soon the horses began staggering.

"We're pushing them too hard," Dani cried. "We've got to pace them or they'll drop."

They still had several miles before they'd reach the higher foothills where most of the citizens of Denver had gathered. Matt reluctantly agreed with Dani. In fact, he went her one better. "Get down," he said. "Whisk can get his wind back faster if we're not in the saddle."

Dani didn't tell Matt about the bump on her head. She still felt rotten, but she jogged along beside Matt, who was leading the two horses.

The crowd of people they had been keeping pace with soon outdistanced them. Matt and Dani would be the last ones to reach safety—if they reached it at all.

Herbie still had to bear Brian's weight, but at least the horse didn't have to gallop at full speed.

Matt and Dani stayed on foot for ten minutes, both of them focused on the northwest, looking for any sign of the flood that they knew would soon be upon them. They didn't see anything, so they continued to jog, giving the horses as much of a breather as they could.

Suddenly Whisk and Herbie were anxious to gallop. They felt something, heard something, or knew something instinctively. And Matt and Dani didn't question it.

They leapt back up onto Whisk and raced as fast as the horse could manage. Herbie was right behind them. The breather had helped. They were making good time.

But not quite good enough.

A few moments later Matt and Dani heard what had spooked the horses. Low, at first, it sounded like the rumble of a noisy air conditioner. Then it grew steadily louder until it seemed more like the roar of a jet engine up close. At that point the ground began to shake as if a big truck were driving down a small and narrow street. Only this shaking didn't stop. It got worse.

"I see it!" Dani yelled fearfully. She pointed up into the mountains. A fast-moving brown wall of muck filled the entire space between two mountain peaks! It was sloshing across the top of the northern foothills on its journey down to Denver.

The tidal wave was just a couple of miles north of them. The northern foothills were smothered beneath hundreds of millions of tons of mud and water, which then continued to flow southeast.

By the time it came out of the mountains, the brown river of death was at least one hundred and fifty feet deep and six miles wide. And Matt and Dani were still in its path.

"We've got to get to higher ground!" Dani shouted.

They were alone, racing against nature's revenge. Above them, on a steep hill, some of the nearly six hundred people who had fled Denver were shouting their encouragement.

Matt and Dani called out to Whisk and Herbie, urging them on. The wall of mud and water appeared to be less than a mile away, and it was moving much faster than they were.

144

The horses were at the limit of their endurance, yet they struggled up the hill. They lurched and fought for every yard, every foot, every inch. Finally, though, the animals were near the point of collapse.

The westernmost edge of the tidal wave was almost on top of them.

Matt and Dani jumped off Whisk's back and pulled at the reins of both straining horses.

"Come on, you can do it!" Dani exclaimed.

"Don't give up!" cried Matt.

The freezing-cold river of slime hit Whisk and Herbie low on their legs. The horses nearly lost their footing, but neither Matt nor Dani would let go of the reins—even though they were in danger of being dragged into the brown death. The horses had saved them and they wanted to save the horses in return. And then there was Brian who was still on Herbie's back.

With Matt and Dani steadying them, Whisk and Herbie frantically kicked against the earth beneath the mud and water that flowed hard against their legs. In a final push, they jumped out of the edge of the brown tidal wave and stood quivering, safe and alive.

The crowd at the top of the hill erupted into wild cheers. Matt and Dani hugged their horses. And then Matt and Dani hugged each other—neither wanting to let the other go.

_____ Chapter 23 _____

THE CHEERING DIED DOWN AS THE CITIZENS OF DENVER stood silently and watched the tidal wave of mud and water wash over their city, burying it forever.

A city, however, isn't a bunch of buildings. It's the people. And except for those few who had decided that Matt's warning was a false alarm, the rest of the population had survived. They would go somewhere else, and instead of living off the wreckage of their old city, they would build a new one. They had no choice.

Brian walked hesitantly over to the campfire where Matt and Dani sat huddled against the night. The river of mud was still flowing below them, and they listened to its steady roar.

"Hey, I hope I'm not interrupting anything," said Brian, forcing a laugh.

Dani quickly rose to her feet and Brian took an involuntary step backward. But then Dani gently took Brian's arm and walked with him away from the fire.

Matt couldn't hear anything they were saying. . . .

"There are four things I want to tell you," Brian began. "The first is that you're about the neatest girl I've ever known. The second is that I deserved that clunk on the head I got—I apologize for being a dunce. The third is that I want to thank you for getting me out of Denver. And the fourth is that I hope you'll stay with me. We're all thinking of heading south together. We figure we'll set up a new Denver down near where Pueblo used to be. Will you come?"

Matt could just make them out in the shadows of the firelight. Brian and Dani were standing close together. Then they hugged and it looked as if they exchanged a kiss.

Matt's heart sank.

When Dani came back to the fire and sat down next to him, Matt grimly said, "As soon as Herbie is in shape to travel, I'll be heading to California."

Dani's eyes sparkled.

"I suppose," Matt continued softly, unsure of himself, "that you'll be staying with these people."

Dani giggled.

"What's so funny?" he asked suspiciously.

"I was just thinking that we'd met at this camp-out and we got to talking. And here I was, kind of hoping you'd ask me out for a date."

It was the old familiar game. Were they playing it for the last time? he wondered.

Matt didn't look at her. He stared into the fire and said, "I'd like to ask you out, but I'm afraid I'm leaving town. Would you like to go out anyway?"

"Depends," she said coyly.

"On what?"

"If I'm moving to the same place you're moving to."

Matt stared at her. "California," he said in a whisper.

"Hey, me, too!" she cried. "What a coincidence. We can have a beach date. I think I'd really like that. Just imagine, the two of us riding horses along the surf, just like in a TV commercial."

A big, broad smile broke across Matt's face. "I know where we can get the horses."

They talked about their fantasy date: swimming, lying in the sun, and rubbing suntan oil on each other's back. Then they talked about watching the sun set into the Pacific, walking hand and hand back to a home that neither one of them had.

"I'd walk you to your door," Matt said.

"And I'd tell you what a great time I had." Dani paused, thinking about the note Matt had left her that morning, and then she added, "I'd tell you that I was hoping we'd go out on another date real soon. You know, I wouldn't want to lose you."

"I wouldn't want to lose you, either."

Dani leaned close to him. "We'd be standing there

and I'd look up at you expectantly, waiting for the perfect end to our date. . . .

Matt took a deep breath and leaned over and kissed her.

She kissed him back.

They looked at each other for a long moment and then Matt said, "Best date I never had."

"Hey, I was going to say that!"

Two days later Matt and Dani said their good-byes and set off together to cross the Rockies. The majestic peaks of the great mountain range matched their soaring spirits. They were on their way again. Together. Maybe, in the end, that was all that really mattered.

Further titles from Methuen

While every effort is made to keep prices low, it is sometimes necessary to increase prices at short notice. Methuen reserve the right to show new retail prices on covers which may differ from those previously advertised in the text or elsewhere.

The prices shown below were correct at the time of going to press.

All these books are available at your bookshop or newsagent, or can be ordered direct from the publisher. Just tick the titles you want and fill in the form below.

METHUEN BOOKS Cash Sales Department
P.O. Box 11, Falmouth,
Cornwall TR10 9EN

Please send cheque or postal order, no currency, for purchase price quoted and allow the following for postage and packing;

UK	60p for the first book, 25p for the second book and 15p for each additional book ordered to a maximum charge of £1.90.
BFPO and Eire	60p for the first book, 25p for the second book and 15p for each next seven books, thereafter 9p per book.
Overseas Customers	£1.25 for the first book, 75p for the second book and 28p for each subsequent title ordered.

NAME (Block letters) ....

ADDRESS ....

....